The Gentle Eye

Ron Mueller

The Gentle Eye

Books and Stories by Ron Mueller

The Door Series
The Door
Aliens We
The Endless Hole
The Swarm
Esoteric Journey
The Gentle Eye

The Taelo Series
Taelo: The Early Years
Taelo: The Golden Feather
Taelo: Journey of Discovery
Taelo: Dangerous Passage
Taelo: Condor Clan Slingers
Taelo: Circumvention
Taelo: The Journey of Sages
Taelo: Collection
Taelo: Future Leaders Journey

A Taelo Story:
White Swan and Quiet Pheasant
The Child's Name
Floating Cloud
Quiet Rabbit
Busy Bee
Little Otter & Talking Wren
Broken Spear
Burley Bear & Meadow Flower
A Taelo Story Collection

Science Fiction
The Savitar Series:
Journey's End
Savitar
Confluence
Savitar Collection

Bram Nielson Series
The Fold
The Message
Fold Wormhole
Negative Fold
Ripples in Time
Bram Nielson Collection

Single Science Fiction Books:
Current Past and Future
The Event
Viajante 7

Ron Mueller

Fiction Series

The Alex Evercrest Series
The River Front
The Girl on The Grill
Missing
Maggot
Racist
Votive Candles
Windy City
Country Road
Pool of Blood
Sins of the Daughter
Alex Evercrest Heroin Collection
Body Parts
The Skull Collector
The Vanishing
The Shadow Fighter
Moonshine
Grief's Trajectory
The Magic Touch
Northern Lights
Alex Evercrest Collection Two
New Direction
A Family Affair

A Brian Oneil Novell
Hawaiian Phoenix
Moon Curser
Death Broker
Hawaiian Princesses

The Problem Solver Series
Solutions
Drug Lords
Border Crosser

Imagination by Courtney Huynh and Chloe Parker

The Gentle Eye
By: *Ron Mueller*

Around the World Publishing LLC
4914 Cooper Road Suite 144
Cincinnati, Ohio 45242-9998

The Gentle Eye © 2025

ISBN 13: 978-1-68223-929-2
ISBN 10: 1-68223-929-2

Distributed by Ingram
Cover Picture by: adike @ShutterStock
Cover Design by: Ron Mueller

Ron Mueller

The Gentle Eye

Table of Content

Ron Mueller

1

The Enigmatic Problem

Before I get into describing the enigmatic problem and the enigmatic person that is pursuing it, let me introduce myself. I am Laki, a humble and, as I have learned during my interactions with The Admiral and his Cosmos team, a really poor historian of the people of the planet Maraburo who have named me their global Historian. I am now also a member of United Intergalactic Worlds Organization, an honor I probably don't deserve. This organization brings all the worlds that the enigmatic person, Five Star Admiral Joseph Pender Elsinger, and his Cosmos team discovered as they tracked down the worlds populated by humans. I refer to him as "The Admiral" and I am continuously humbled by his pursuit of the answers to questions that I as a historian should have asked and failed to do so. He and his team from Earth traveled the Universe to validate the theory that the population on Earth had been seeded there thousands of years ago by a humans. His team theorized that based on how the ancient pyramids of Giza were built, the base provided the locations of eight seeded planets and the top of the pyramid represented the ninth planet that did the seeding.

1 The Enigmatic Problem

That theory was beyond the shadow of conventional thinking and well into the realm of the occult for the historians of Earth. I admit that I would have been among the doubters but as a citizen of the ninth planet I am a testament to the correctness of the theory that the Admiral and his team set out to prove.

He led his team on an <u>Esoteric Journey</u> in search of those planets and eventually came to my planet; the ninth planet and the one that had seeded the other eight. He found a planet that had suffered historic dementia. I an eminent and celebrated historian of Maraburo, had no clue about the history that I had so eloquently written about. I documented the Admiral's Esoteric Journey, and I am now going to narrate his continuing esoteric journey to answer a question that he has challenged his team with and a question that personally leaves me mystified.

That question is "WHY?."

Why did my home planet seed the other eight planets?

WHY?

I learned that the Admiral had latched onto this question and decided that it was a critical one that needed answering. He postulated that the resources required for a feat such as traveling across the universe would have weighed heavy on any population. There had to be more than a popular social desire driving such a venture. He theorized that there was a threat that had united my entire ancient kin. His theory was that it had to be the threat of extinction.

The Gentle Eye

This meant that the ancient people of Maraburo had knowledge of such a threat and that they took it seriously enough to commit the resources to distribute the human seed across the universe to ensure its continued existence. He was sure it was the drive for human survival.

As I stated, I am a historian and when I learned about his theory, I was baffled about the fact that in all the documents that I had perused I never ran across any mention of such a threat. That caused me to ask the same question.

Why?

Indeed, that question frustrated me.

The Admiral asked me that question in a slightly different way. He had asked me why the Maraburo ancients had constructed the behemoth spaceship the Kodho that had seeded the other eight planets. He asked what had driven the scientist to design a spaceship that could reach the speed of light? I had grown up with the Kodho orbiting the planet and had never asked those questions with the same passion that he put them to me.

I embarrassingly looked down at the floor like a delinquent student that had not done his homework and answered that I had no clue. The thought that went through my mind was that I was negligent in doing my research. I had reached into the tree of history and had chosen to write about the low hanging events that were easily harvested. I had not reached high enough to reach the grand history of my people. I personally saw that as my failure.

1 The Enigmatic Problem

I knew then that the Admiral because of his persistent drive he would be the one that would discover the details that would be found on the highest branches of Maraburo's historical tree. I knew that he would keep digging until he could answer the question:

WHY?

****

The visit to Maraburo had created a question that would not leave Joe's mind. The use of the giant seeding spaceship Kodho to save the people on Niam from their dying sun had overshadowed his need to answer the question but once that historic accomplishment of saving the five billion people was done, the question of Why returned to constantly bedevil and prod his mind like the shock of a cattle prod. He became driven by the need to answer that question.

He held a work session with his team and asked them the question. But he asked them in terms that would cause them to want to give him a solid answer. He asked them what would make them give up everything they had, all their worldly goods and even their lives to accomplish something that they knew would not immediately benefit them.

The silence that followed made him think that he had not asked the right question. He was about to ask the question another way but then Lacey spoke up quietly.

Lacey began by saying that this was the first time she had thought about such a situation. She then said that she would do it to save the rest of the people in the room.

She was greeted with silence.

The Gentle Eye

Joe was surprised when Darian said that was the only thing that would make sense to him. He added that he had so many people to whom he owed his life that he would most likely include all of them as well. He would do it to save his world. The world he knew.

That seemed to open up the flood gates from the rest of the team and the general sentiment coalesced around the concept of saving those around them and those they loved.

Joe nodded and then asked what would have caused the Maraburoans to support the use of all their resources to seed the eight planets with their children, friends, and themselves. What possibly could have caused that to happen. He added that there was no evidence of any massive destruction on the planet. He pointed out that there seemed to be no threat.

Lydia was quick to answer that it had to be a threat to the entire population of the planet. It had to be a threat that they all believed was very close to happening. She shook her head and said that it had to be something so obvious that anyone exposed to it would understand and would believe.

Yara nodded and said that she agreed but that kind of information should have come out in their review of the historic records that they had been pouring over.

H^3 agreed but he reminded everyone that they were the ones that had opened the door to a past that the Maraburoans had totally forgotten and the records that were the basis of their knowledge had all come from the computers on the derelict spaceship the Kodho. He doubted all of the history of the planet was on its computer.

1 The Enigmatic Problem

Samantha reminded everyone that they had so far not found any records on the planets that went back to the time the Kodho had been built and the thousands of years it had spent seeding the eight planets. They had not tapped into the flow of the sap that would give them the sweet syrup that they could put on their the layers of Maraburoan historical pancakes.

Darian chuckled and said that his mate talked in such an eloquent way because she was anxious to get to her beloved Vermont maple trees and get to the sap that was currently filling the tubs so she could put it over the fire where she would make her delicious syrup. He smiled and said that he agreed with her that the team's knowledge was based on only having read one chapter of the book of Maraburoan history.

Joe smiled and said that springtime was also having an effect on him, and he wanted to be on the ranch and help with the birthing of the new calves. He said that he would continue to work on a way to answer the question of, WHY and he wanted to have the team focus on that question but added that they all deserved a break after having drained their souls saving of the people now relocated to Nivian.

He announced a two week leave for everyone.

Linda announced that she and Tom were heading to their home in London to be there for the Christening of their newest granddaughter and planned to spend some time touring the first two planets that the team had discovered.

Joe wished them a good trip. He then reminded the team that three new spherical ships were nearing completion and would soon be ready to be commissioned. He added that the three captains for those ships were all in the room and since he wanted no confusion he was letting them all officially know that Lacey, Yara and Samantha would be the captains for the three new ships. He suggested that they tour the three ships and decide which ship each of them wanted and what they wanted to name their ship.

He watched as Lydia joined the other three captains to congratulate them on their new commands. He knew that the next voyage would have a different character to it because the four would be operating from four separate vessels versus all being on one ship and sharing the role of captain. He had discussed this for hours with Lydia to make sure she was in fine remaining as the Captain of the ISF Cosmos Terra.

Lydia had assured him that she loved the Terra and as long as he made it his command ship she was pleased to be its captain. She had let him know that Lacey, Yara and Samantha had discussed the three new ships nearing completion and had agreed to the use the sequence of the planets that had been discovered as the names for the new ships. She had pointed out that Samantha was the exception.

Lacey had asked to have her ship name to be the ISF Cosmos Nivian after the planet that the second discovered group of humans had now been relocated to. She felt that she had a very close association with the entire population that she had been a part of saving.

1 The Enigmatic Problem

Yara had asked to have her ship's name to be the ISF Cosmos Gaja. The third discovered planet.

Samantha said that she wanted to see if she could skip out a couple of planets and be allowed to take the name of the planet where a love affair that had caught her imagination was in progress. She wanted to name her ship the ISF Cosmos Kelima because she knew she wanted to embrace her love affair with her new ship in the same manner as the love affair on the new leaders of Kelima.

Joe agreed to allow a couple of planets to be skipped and that each of the three now needed to select which of the three spheres they wanted to claim.

Lydia chuckled and said that she had toured the three and they were duplicates of the Terra and she was sure that the three would have no problem accepting the helm of any of the three new ones.

She waited until they were both back on the ranch walking across the field to go fishing to discuss Joe's intense focus on the question of Why. She asked what was it about the Maraburo history that concerned him..

Joe pointed at one of the steers that had a calf following it. He said that if a wolf came out of the woods, the mother steer would put herself between the calf and the wolf. He figured that seeding eight planets was like the mother steer. He then described the scene of a herd of elephants where every adult faced an oncoming pride of lions and put the young behind them.

The ancient Maraburoans had done that for the human race. But why had they done it kept nagging him. Where was the wolf, where was the pride of lions, what was the threat?

He felt that the answer to why, given the space travel time, was still very critical to answer. He pointed out that Tom and Linda had given them the ability to move from star to star, from galaxy to galaxy and traverse the universe in mere hours so it was hard to comprehend a threat that might still be on its way toward the seeding planet and that was what he was concerned with. He felt that the answer to Why would let them get one step ahead of any threat that might in fact still be on its way towards Maraburo. The Maraburoans had spread the human race out across the universe to shield it and had left themselves exposed to a threat that might still be on the way.

Lydia nodded and said that what they needed was to find the records that the Maraburoans must have hidden somewhere on the planet.

Joe nodded as he cast his fishing line and felt the hit of the first catch of the morning. He figured he and his team needed to spend time to physically search the planet for the needle hidden in a planetary haystack.

It did not take long for he and Lydia to be carrying enough trout and a couple of bass back to the house. They both knew that Uncle Ted would insist on cleaning the fish and would sent them to relax with a cup of tea on the veranda while he fixed lunch.

1 The Enigmatic Problem

Life on the ranch had a cadence that seemed to always be in step with what Joe and Lydia needed when they were not out traversing the universe.

2

Return to Maraburo

I Laki, was still on the ISF Cosmos Javelin, in orbit around Jomaoko, participating in establishing the United Intergalactic Worlds Organization. This was a privilege that I knew that I did not deserve but nonetheless was overjoyed to be a part of. Because I was the representative from Maraburo, the seeding planet, representatives from the other eight planets treated me with a veneration that was embarrassing. They had no clue that I was the most ignorant among them. I and my planet had forgotten the seeding.

But let me turn my focus to what I did when I learned what the Admiral was planning on his return trip to Maraburo. The fact that he wanted to search the planet for the missing portion of history that I had overlooked was the strongest pull that I have ever felt. I could not wait to participate in such a search.

The question that came to my mind was how could a repository of historic importance not have been discovered during the thousands of years that had passed since the time of the seeding. It seemed impossible that such a thing could have happened.

2 Return to Maraburo

I was surprised when the Admiral arrived with three additional spaceships. The fact that they were duplicates and brandished both heavy armament as well as a wealth of what appeared to be telescopes and other sensors was impressive. I was struct with the speed and ability that the Cosmos organization displayed in so rapidly expanding their fleet.

The Maraburo leadership were nervous when the Admiral's four vessels took very strategic orbits around the planet. They worried about his intentions.

Having just returned from the meeting that was focused on how the nine human worlds and the other five non-human worlds would all work together in a harmonious, friendly, and productive way, I reassured them that the Admiral had no ill intentions.

It was not long after his arrival that the Admiral asked to address the Leadership Council. There was a very different situation for this address. Since the previous time when only I and the Council leader had the neural mind head gear, enough copies of the head gear had been made so that the Admiral would be communicating to all of the council at the same time. This greatly improved the interaction between he, the captain of the four spaceships, and the entire council membership. It allowed me to focus on what the Admiral's intent was.

He presented the fact that he had spent many hours since his last visit struggling over the reason Why the entire planet of Maraburo would have spent what had to have been an enormous effort and absorbed an astronomical cost to seed eight additional planets with humans but there was no record of it.

He made the very rational point the Maraburo forefathers must have identified a monumental and very believable threat to the race and had decided to safeguard the human race by spreading it across the universe. They had acted like a mother shielding her child. The Maraburoans of that time willingly had put the human race throughout the universe to protect it while they had stayed behind to face the threat. He then made the point that the threat had yet to materialize.

He pointed out that the effort, technological development, and cost of developing a spaceship the size of the Kodho must have strained the engineers, the technologists and drained all the resources of the time. He then asked a question that should have been one that I should have researched and had an answer for.

Where was the knowledge currently hidden on Maraburo?

He then asked for permission for his team to search for that knowledge. He pointed out that direct contact between his team and the people on Maraburo was not yet cleared so he wanted to have a team on the planet with which to work.

He asked for a ground team consisting of people knowledgeable of the planet's geology, geography, architecture, engineering, and history to find out what had driven the Maraburo forefathers to take the extreme measure of seeding the eight planets and then hiding the information of having done so.

He made the point that once they had that information they would know the WHY the seeding was necessary and why they felt a need to hide the information about such an activity.

He closed by restating that the threat to Maraburo might still be in transit coming at it at close to the speed of light and that time was the currency that was currently being spent aimlessly by the Maraburoans that had lost the connection to the monumental effort of carrying out the seeding.

I was surprised to once again be asked by the Leadership Council to take the lead and assemble the teams that were being asked for.

It was not so much of a request by the leadership team but an order to select the best minds in each of the fields and to select as many people needed to make the search successful and rapid.

In reality I was one of the least qualified to do such a thing. I was sure that some of the writers of fiction and fantasy were more qualified than I. At least they were using their imagination to create stories that were entertaining when everything that I had written about history was not only somewhat boring but in most part totally wrong. All I as a historian had done to date was to write fiction about history and was now being asked to correct that story.

Again, I have wandered off course, and I realize that not only am I a terrible historian, but I also have trouble concentrating on the task of narrating the actions taken by the Admiral.

Before I was able to pull the teams together I needed to ask what specialty the Admiral was asking for.

He had a linguistics specialist, Kashanti work with me to clarify what each specialty was. Having the mental connection made the going easier but it was still a challenge.

This was a great exercise for me in that Kashanti and I needed to learn more about each other's language before we made any headway. Doing so was a mental game similar to moving a ball through three dimensional space only the neural head gear allowed us to do it in each other's mind.

He thought what a geologist did, and I would then think a Ayikungban or ground tracker.

He thought what a person specializing in geography did and I was able to think of a Didedide or maker of maps.

He thought what an architect did, and I then knew that person would be a Ziquratum.

Then it came my turn. I have mentioned multiple times that I am a historian. In my language I am referred to as a Ragegita. That first thing that registered in Kashanti's mind was it was one to be mocked. I burst out laughing because that was probably an appropriated perspective of how I should be treated.

2 Return to Maraburo

Once I had what skill each member needed to have, it turned out that the difficulty was not identifying a sufficient number of participants but one of sorting through the resumes of ten times the number of people that were needed. I approached that task by selecting one person that was a recognized leader in the field and asked them to select the right number of people based on the areas that their team would be searching for the information treasure the Admiral was looking for.

The Admiral asked me to convene those leaders so he could create a team that included people on the four spheres he had orbiting Maraburo. He stated that he was looking to create a team that would work well together and could move swiftly.

I convened those leaders, and we went on a learning journey that amazed us and created a camaraderie that was truly life changing.

There were five of us that would lead the ground search and there would be an on board member that would pair with each of us.

The Admiral had each of us introduce ourselves and our skill sets.

He then shared that he planned to scour the planet and find the knowledge repository and to do that he needed a ground team that was sufficient to do the work rapidly. He emphasized that he felt that speed was urgent.

Once each of the leaders on the planet had introduced themselves and the matching personnel on the spheres had done the same, the Admiral let us know that he was going to visually present the preparation that the four Cosmos Spheres had done before returning to Maraburo.

He shared that he wanted everyone to be at the same level of understanding and appreciation of how important he thought it was to find the answer to the Why question.

The presentation and the Admirals insistence that the four Cosmos ships be able to react to any obstacle that they might face was an amazing demonstration that impressed all of us Maraburoan. He had a thousand steel balls the size of bowling balls randomly launched in the path of the four ships and had them fly through at flank speed as the last test before returning to Maraburo. I and all team members on Maraburo viewed the video of that flight and we were amazed that the four ships flew through the randomly flying steel balls and none were hit. It looked like it was a game in a circus arcade where the targets randomly appear, and the shooter has to react instantly.

When the video ended I realized that I and everyone on Maraburo had been holding their breath. It was then that I came to the realization that I would never be qualified to be a captain of a spaceship and I most likely would not be qualified to be a crew member. I laughed as I wondered if I would even be able to qualify as a sous chef in the kitchen.

The presentation had nothing to do with the actual search, but it made everyone appreciate how serious the Admiral was about finding the information that would answer his question of Why. Every member voiced their support for such a search.

****

2 Return to Maraburo

During the time Joe was waiting for the three new Cosmos ships to be finished, commissioned and ready to run through their qualification exercises he spent his time back on the ranch participating in the annual cattle branding season. Branding had been replaced with tagging the new cattle with ear tags. The change was not because of preventing pain to the calf or to the cattle but an economic one of having a more valuable hide later when they were butchered.

It was a great way for him to physically work hard, enjoy every meal and sleep tight. However, this time what seemed to consume him was that nagging question of Why the ancient Maraburoans had hidden the reason they had seeded eight planets spread across multiple galaxies. He had to constantly be reminded to clip the tag on the ear that was being held out to him.

One of the younger cowhands laughingly said that he wanted to get done by dinner and pushed him away and took over the tagging operation.

Joe got the message and went riding out on the plain.

He asked the Why question of everyone participating in the tagging, every person around the dinner table and of Lydia when they talked in bed or were riding, fishing of skinny dipping in their favorite pond.

Uncle Ted's and his father's answers seemed to resonate with him the best. Uncle Ted figured that the bad guys were on the way and the Maraburoans wanted to protect the eight seeded planets.

His father agreed and added that by erasing the information from the record they in fact would most likely also protect the home planet population.

Lydia agreed with both of them and said that what she was curious about was how the ancient Maraburoans had successfully erased the information and why they preserved the spaceship, the Kodho. She speculated that their speed of light spaceship must have cost a monumental amount and that it also provided a way for the Maraburoans to save at least a portion of the population if they faced a planetary destruction event.

Joe then asked everyone where they would hide something so that it would be next to impossible to find.

He got, the deepest part of the ocean, buried under some glacier, or buried under some mountain.

Over dinner, between bites of her steak, Lydia suggested that she would hide it in plain sight. She would put it on the top of the empire state building or in the torch of the statue of liberty or the tallest building in the world.

Joe absorbed everyone's input and by the time the three ships were ready for their trial runs, he was ready to get back to Maraburo to search for that information treasure. He was almost certain that the human race still faced a formidable threat.

Every one of the Captains knew that they were in for grueling space aerobics training with their newly commissioned space spheres.

2 Return to Maraburo

As the ships went through their grueling trial runs, Joe realized that the crews of all four ships not only became proficient, but he felt that they reached a level of performance that in combination would make them nearly invincible.

He surprised his four captains by having the Kodho join them. He had reassigned Captain Jeffery Yang to be the Captain of the Kodho and had transferred his entire team from the Cosmos Empowerer with him. The Kodho had also gone through intensive exercises and though it could not dance like the four spheres the giant ship had demonstrated a capability that surprised both Joe and Captain Yang.

Once the five ships were ready, he gave the order to travel through the Hole to Maraburo.

Lydia was in overall Command of the Cosmos Ships and took them through the hole following their normal procedure. The Kodho was the last ship through the hole and seemed to be chasing the four seemingly small spheres.

Joe then had the four spheres take up orbits that would give the four a total view of the planet at all times. This would allow the entire planet to get scrutinized by the sensors that the ships possessed.

He had the Kodho take up the orbit that it had been in for more than ten thousand years before he had requested that it become part of his command.

His initial focus was to establish a ground team of Maraburoans. He had the four captains identify the appropriate people to pair with the Maraburoans who would be their ground crew. He wanted the teams to as rapidly as possible find the historic record that would answer his question of Why.

He asked Tom and Linda to lead the ground search.

He had H^3 and Darian lead the ocean search.

He then asked each Captain what teams they wanted to lead.

Samantha volunteered to lead the search of the Northern Ice Cap and several of the Northern glaciers.

Yara volunteered to lead the search of the Southern Ice Cap and the Southern glaciers.

Lacey said that she and Lydia had agreed to search the cities.

When Jeffrey asked which team he should join, Joe said that he wanted him to take the Kodho out and learn how to maneuver it at the speed of light the way he had maneuvered the Empowerer.

Jeffrey laughed and said that at the speed of light the Kodho would be lucky to wiggle but he would see what he could get it to do.

That got a good luck from the other four captains. Each of them had been at the helm of the Kodho when it reached the speed of light and they all knew that it was great in a straight flight.

Lydia had flown it as she tried to outrun the explosion of the red sun and knew that the Kodho was a magnificent ship, and she had stressed it beyond its design, and she had guided it in a long turn as she tried escape that sun's heat wave. She suggested that he try maneuvers at less than the speed of light and work his way up to it.

2 Return to Maraburo

Joe surprised Elisha Sands by promoting her and reassigning her to the Kodho as the lead technical officer. He smiled and let her know that he was sure that she could use her skills to make the Kodho dance. He knew that she was the reason that Lydia had been able to outrun the heat blast bubble from the dying red sun.

He hoped that later he would be rewarded for having promoted her.

He then ordered that the search begin in earnest.

3

Search for the Treasure

I, Laki, overall leader of the Maraburo's ground teams in search of its ancient secrets that the Admiral sought so he could have a definite answer to Why my ancient ancestors had seeded eight other planets across the universe and then hidden that reason was constantly surprised by what had remained hidden from the population. I am recognized as one of the leading historians of my planet and almost on a daily basis my ignorance was further exposed.

I watched Tom, Linda, H^3 and Darian work together to search both land and sea for some construct that might be the repository of the information that the Admiral was seeking. They used satellites to scour the land with a variety of sensors and had autonomous underwater vehicles built and programmed to search the sea floor with sonar and cameras using a variety of frequencies. They found many ancient structures that had remained hidden because no one had ever looked for them.

On land they found a seed repository meant to provide a way to reestablish plant life should a global catastrophe happen.

3 Search for the Treasure

In the sea they found several ancient, submerged cities that had been lost because the continental plates had sunk down. On the sea floors they found immeasurable wealth of polymetallic nodules of cobalt, copper, nickel, manganese, zinc, silver, and gold.

I have stated everything in proper English but the interaction of Earth English and Maraburoan Bekee created some humorous moments as the teams in space communicated with the Maraburoan teams on the planet. It was not only humorous, but it was clear that the teams were not only operating at a high serious level, but they were also enjoying learning about each other.

It turned out that Samantha and Yara and the two teams on the planet teamed up and worked together in the search of the northern and southern ice caps and glaciers. They used devices similar to sonar to peer beneath the ice caps in areas where the ice was miles in depth. Almost two miles down they found a huge structure that once they tunneled down to it they discovered the ancient records of the development that led up to the construction of the Kodho.

I was the one responsible to share these discoveries with the leadership council. It proved hard to keep myself from denigrating myself for having been so ignorant of the history and the accomplishments of my ancestors.

It was clear to me that many of the leadership council had come to the conclusion that the top thinkers on the planet had failed to capture the greatness of the Maraburoan ancestors. They began to ask for specific names of some of the past sages that had produced those accomplishments. They wanted to publicly recognize them.

The Gentle Eye

The most interesting search turned out to be led by Captains Lydia and Lacey. The team they led examined the most likely hiding places where top secret information might be hidden. They were interested in the oldest structures that existed on Maraburo. This proved to be a tour of all the famous buildings, learning their historic status, touring the water gardens, and several via duct water transport systems that traversed dry areas of the planet. They were looking in what I thought of places too obvious to hide something as important as to the reason why the eight planets had been seeded.

The detail by which they examined such sites provided insights to construction methods, materials, and the ingenious use of engineering principles by those ancient personnel. It also accented the point in the development of the Maraburoan world when a decision to protect the environment had caused the choice of using sophisticated tunneling methods to connect the cities versus building surface connectivity took place.

The surprise came when the most famous and highest structure on Maraburo, the "Spire to the stars" was examined. This took the entire time that all the searches were taking place because the spire was a structure that could not be easily accessed. It was at the center of the capital and rose up from the center of the ellipse shaped park in front of the Building of the Leadership. It was then that I learned that the "Spire to the Stars" had been built before the buildings that now surrounded it. The elliptical shape of the drive to the front of the building had been deliberately designed such that for all points on the curve, the sum of the two distances to the focal points is a constant.

3 Search for the Treasure

Suddenly it became clear that the ancients had created a structure that deliberately pointed to the top of the spire. The searchers would have found the crystal memory cube that held the answer much sooner had they been able to get to it without the need to manufacture the hover craft allowing the very top golden sphere to be accessed.

Captains Linda, Lydia, and their ground team were the ones that found the message from the ancients that held the answer to the Admiral's question of "Why."

I have been remiss by not highlighting the personal efforts that the Admiral had personally embark on. He began looking for a star system that was within the time frame that would fit with the decision to seed the planets. He was looking for any fast moving object that was coming through space towards Maraburo. He formulated the concept but then engaged Tom, Linda and H^3 to develop a search routine that scanned space around Maraburo's star, Kpakpan in an ever enlarging spherical search for any very fast approaching object. Once it was activated and he was confident it was working the way he had envisioned it would he waited as the program and the telescopic sensors did their work. He discovered Why the Ancient Maraburoans had taken action to counteract the threat of the annihilation of the inhabitants of Maraburo before they had seeded the planets.

There indeed was a threat of total annihilation still on its way.

The answer to Why is a story that has enriched the foundation of Maraburo's history to the point that it has totally changed the attitudes and nature of its current population. Maraburoans are only four billion people strong and one of the least populated planets of the nine human planets, but we are now sixty forty billion proud because that is the number of people that we have protected.

So let me refocus on the actions taken by the Admiral and all the discoveries that enriched Maraburoan history and brought it to a new level and allowed me as a historian to truly learn how ignorant I had been.

****

Joe had launched the search for the container or repository where the information he sought was being kept. He also thought about what his actions would have been had he been in charge of responding to a physical threat to the planet. What came to mind was to counter the threat. He would have used whatever resources and technology was available to put a protective shield between the planet and any perceived in coming threat. He would have then established a planet wide effort to advance the sciences and the weaponry of the day.

He was sure that the development of the speed of light travel that resulted in the building of the seeding ship the Kodho had to have followed after they had learned of the threat they faced. This thinking led to his establishing a spherical space search for any very fast moving objects that were coming at Maraburo or flying away from it.

3 Search for the Treasure

He knew that he needed the help of the three people he thought of as the genius three: Linda, Tom and H^3. He asked them to write a search program that would guide the ships telescopes and any other pertinent sensors in a spherical search of the space around the Kpakpan star. They were to search for any very fast moving objects coming towards the planet.

He became the person who on a daily basis checked what that search might be yielding. He was also keeping track of all the search teams that were working to find the information that would answer his question of Why. The days led into weeks and then into months. He encouraged his teams to continue with vigor and speed. He meanwhile ran every day as fast as he could on his tread mill and around on the two mile track on the ISF Cosmos Terra as he tried to control his concern for a threat that might still be about to happen.

He took several trips back to Madorite and met with his two Vice Admirals Jorge and Jerry to evaluate the progress being made in making the Cosmos base fully functional. It was during one of these trips that he decided that he was going to establish a cattle ranch there. He, Jorge, and Jerry took a flight out over the vast desert and mountains and located a breath taking area that had several secluded canyons, small but running streams and three stunning mountains that did not have snow caps but instead had green caps that turned out to be trees similar to pines growing on them. He called the ranch he was setting up "Green Caps" and put markers up at the corners of the ranch.

He then asked Jorge to arrange to have the cattle that he was going to send out from his father's ranch to be acclimated on their arrival and then transported to a specific canyon that had a small lake at its center surrounded by wild grasses.

It was on the following trip away from Maraburo back to his father's ranch that he enrolled his father and Uncle Ted in establishing the Three Green Caps Ranch.

He was pleased that both of them embraced the idea of setting up a ranch on Madorite. His father said that he would select the best of his young heifers to send there to start the herd. He figured he could start with a thousand head and within a few years have a respectable size herd going.

He asked whether there would be a market for the beef. Joe smiled and said that was an area that he had not considered but he was sure that Jorge would be interested in getting that set up for the Cosmos personnel that were living on the planet. Whether there was a market for beef on Nivian remained to be discovered.

Uncle Ted smiled and said that he was giving two old men a reason to keep going.

Lydia had kept her focus on her search and had not accompanied Joe, but she had kept track of what he was doing and was dying to see the Three Green Caps ranch.

Joe had shared the huge number of pictures he had taken but she wanted to walk the canyon valley with its jewel blue lake at its center and if there was nothing dangerous in it she wanted to peel off her clothes and take a skinny dip with Joe as they did on almost every visit back to the ranch on which he had grown up.

She wanted to walk the streams and fish for the fish that might exist there, and she wanted to help design the house that she was sure the two of them would build somewhere on the ranch.

It was at the end of her daydreaming that the hover craft attached itself to the high spire in front of the building on Maraburo that was equivalent to the White House. A few moments later it verified that the globe at the top was hollow and that suspended at its center was an object that resembled a four inch crystal cube.

Lydia let out an exuberant yell that stopped all work around her. She knew in her heart that after months of searching she and her team had found what Joe was looking for. She asked that the globe be carefully cut from the top and taken to a lab where the cube would be carefully removed and examined.

It took the rest of the day to bring the top down to ground level and then be transported to a lab that was ready to very carefully remove the cube.

When the cube was finally resting on a surgically clean surface to be examined, she asked if there were any computer readers or other reader types that could hold the crystal cube and extract the information.

When the answer came back a resounding no she arranged for the crystal to be carefully packaged and sent up to the Terra. She then arranged for Linda, Tom, H^3 and Elisha to figure out how to extract the information from the cube.

Elisha took one look at the cube and knew that it was nothing more than an elaborate computer thumb drive or memory storage device. She examined that cube and said that there did not seem to be an in or an out port like that of a traditional computer. She suggested that they set up nine computer connected surfaces that she could hook her computer to that would be placed within a few millimeters of each side of the cube so she could sense what might be internal to the cube.

H^3 asked what she had in mind with such an arrangement.

She responded that what she would be looking for would be energy pulses that put out information utilizing the cubes internal energy.

Linda commented that she doubted the cube generated any internal energy but that the cube would need energy put in to generate those pulses.

Tom suggested putting in light on one surface of the cube to see if that generated an output on any of the other surfaces.

When Elisha asked what frequency of light they should use, Linda pointed to Kpakpan and said that the natural light from the star that Maraburo orbited would be the light she would suggest.

3 Search for the Treasure

The cube was at the center of a lab surrounded by elevated seats surrounding it. Joe, the other captains and on board search team members were all sitting, leaning forward in their seats anticipating what was about to happen. He looked around and realized they were all like spectators, in a tense movie scene or surgical theater, leaning in to make sure they did not miss anything.

Lydia was given the privilege of exposing the first surface of the cube to the Kpakpan light. She removed the shield and exposed the selected cube surface to the rays from Kpakpan. There was total silence as the Elisha's fingers seemed to be playing her keyboard as if she were playing a piano.

Elisha was indeed playing her keyboard and going through every hacking routine she had ever devised. One failure after another passed under her fingertips. She was running out of hacking routines when the routine she had devised to break into the computer on the Kodho started to spew out string after string of computer code. It was a code that she and a ground team had mastered and knew how to parse.

She raised both hands and let out a loud series of Voya, Voya, Voya shouts. The cry was taken up by everyone in the observation seats and though the people participating on Maraburo had no clue what it meant they too took up the cry and that cry continued for enough time that Joe called for silence and asked Elisha what he was cheering for.

Elisha laughed and said that she had no way to know exactly but it was computer code that needed to be read to determine the information that the cube contained. It would require the help of the top IT personnel on Maraburo that she had worked with before. She found it hard to express her jubilation. She then confirmed that the light had gone directly through from the open side to the opposite side by closing off the first side and trying another. She smiled and announced that there would be nine sides of streaming code to decipher.

Joe then directed that he wanted every piece of information held on that cube to be deciphered and stored in enough different locations so that there would be no chance of it ever again being lost.

He then called a meeting to review all the discoveries that seemed to be happening in parallel to each other.

Lydia and Lacey led off by introducing the team players on Maraburo who they credited with doing the hard work of doing the physical discoveries. They also credit them with helping develop and produce the hover craft that the they had used to gain access to where the cube had been found. Each of the ground members were asked to present a pieced of how the search had been conducted. This set the tone for the rest of the meeting by having presented the information in the manner that they had.

3 Search for the Treasure

Tom, Linda, H[3] and Darian followed their lead and had the ground team leader share what they had discovered. Their discoveries consisted of a hidden seed repository and huge fields of various mineral nodules that littered the ocean floor. The wealth that had been discovered was something that would power the future economic health of Maraburo for the foreseeable future.

Samantha and Yara introduced their team and had the ground team leader shared the finding of a huge complex under the southern ice cap large enough to hold several thousand personnel. They had found paper plans of the design of missiles and precursors to the design of the Kodho. At the end of the report, Yara added that now that they had the routine that would access the computers found in the complex that had been brought to life she was sure that a ton more information would surface. She asked that Elisha, and her team add the deciphering of the code in the computers in the underground complex to their work.

Joe then reported on the most recent discovery that the orbital search engine for any object coming at Maraburo at a high speed had found the needle in the haystack that he had it looking for. He credited Tom, Linda and H[3] for helping him set up the search routine and automating it.

He then shared that what it had found was a surprise. It had found an incoming object that was not aimed at Maraburo but at Kpakpan.

Additionally, it had found an outgoing object bearing down on the incoming object.

He said that using the high end of speeds that could be conventionally produced would indicate that both objects were launched in the time frame prior to the building of the Kodho. He shared that given that time frame they were within a few years of having the two object interact with each other.

He also said that most likely they should be looking for a star and a planet that was about ten light years away where they would find the civilization that sought to destroy another civilization that was light years away and posed no threat to them.

He then said that once they had developed enough understanding about the reactions of the ancient Maraburo leaders he planned to prevent the two missiles from exploding. He planned to turn the attacking missile around and have it head back toward the sending planet.

He added that doing so gave the Cosmos and Maraburo teams the time to dig into what they had discovered. Then he and the Cosmos team would pay a visit to the attacking planet so they could understand how a civilization capable of traveling in space could have such a vile attitude. He wanted to know Why they had taken such a hateful and despicable action.

This time the cry of Voya, Voya, Voya came from the team members on the surface of Maraburo and continued for more than ten minutes.

3 Search for the Treasure

4

The Three Green Caps Ranch

The discovery of the hidden, ancient information about the unprovoked attack by some distance civilization was an amazing piece of Maraburoan history that I, Laki, spent every moment pouring over. I learned that the attacking civilization had sent a probe that passed through the Kpakpan system. The astronomers of the time were able to trace the origin of the probe to its originating launch site. They had sent a message of friendship and a desire to establish communication. They were shocked to learn that the beings that had sent out the probe responded with the message that they knew where the Maraburoan planet was located, and they were sending out their response in the form of a missile that would destroy the star they were circling.

I was shocked.

I asked one of the astronomers why Kpakpan would be the target and learned that it saved the attackers the need to know where Maraburo would be because the star would be much easier to target and destroying it would destroy every planet orbiting it.

This caused me no end of mental stress. I kept trying to understand how a civilization advanced enough to be exploring space could possibly be so devoid of any compassion or congenial feelings. It was so strange that I am still struggling with the fact that I cannot come to closure on the thought that an entire civilization exists that is so self-centered that nothing else matters or has value.

So, I have spent much of my time focused on myself and now must refocus on reporting on what the Admiral is doing. I personally asked what he had in mind to deal with the situation.

He shared that he, unlike the ancient Maraburoans had the technology that would allow him to respond directly to the attacking civilization and he had time on his side because he would be able to neutralize the threat of the incoming missile in such a manner that the missile would be traveling back to the attacking planet.

He also wanted to allow the personnel on Maraburo time to learn about their home planet. During that time, he was going to use the time evaluating how the whole of the human population should respond to such heinous behavior by an entire alien population. The Admiral admitted that he would need all the guidance he could find because he currently could only think of totally eliminating such a population.

It was interesting to me that the Admiral chose to deal with the situation by going to the planet Madorite that had become the headquarters of the Cosmos fleet. It was part of the star system Izulite which also had the planet Nivian where the human population that had been saved from the dying red star was now located.

The Gentle Eye

I personally engaged their representative to the United Intergalactic Worlds Organization and learned that the Admiral and his wife Captain Lydia Tabata were looked at as the two who were instrumental in saving everyone on Nivian and that the leaders there were ecstatic when the Admiral chose to move the Cosmos Command to Madorite a planet in their new star system. His choice to locate to their system was seen as a sign that Nivian has a special place in his heart.

I am trying to share the fact that the Admiral went to Madorite to establish a ranch similar to the one he had grown up on Earth and he had his father and the person that he referred to as Uncle Ted help him set up the ranch. It was a personal endeavor that he and Captain Tabata undertook jointly. When I questioned him on why he had chosen to set up a ranch at a time that did not seem to fit the situation he was facing he laughed and said that it was the only way that he knew how to deal with the situation that had been uncovered on Maraburo.

He needed time to mentally deal with his personal feelings that at the moment were very hostile towards those sending a missile to destroy Kpakpan. He needed time to reaffirm the principles that had guided him throughout his life.

He also needed to be able to transition to a life more removed from Earth so he could focus on the goal of exploring the universe without the politics there hindering him.

He then smiled and said that getting his father and Uncle Ted engaged in setting up a ranch on Madorite made the new ranch have a flavor of the one he grew up on. He added that he hoped that Lydia would love the new ranch as much as he did.

With that understanding I chose to spend every moment that he was gone to educate myself, a historian, on the true history of my planet. I wanted to focus on the rich history of those heroes and heroines whose names I hoped to learn so that I could bring them back into the memories of the people they had sacrificed their lives for.

****

Joe met with the people he took to be those that shared the history of the Cosmos program; Tom, Linda, H³, Yara, Samantha, Jarad, Lacie, Jorge, Jerry, Jeffery, Jackie, Elisha, and Lydia. He shared the fact that he was going to take leave. He made the point that he personally needed time to focus on re-grounding himself on the principles that had guided him throughout his life. He said that the sacrifices that the ancient heroes and heroines of Maraburo had made needed a response that at the moment he could not see himself doing in an honorable way. He let everyone know that he was going to focus on setting up a large ranch on Madorite and was doing so as a therapeutic way to allow him to deal with the situation.

Jackie had wondered why she had been invited to the meeting but then realized that Joe was letting her see how he was mentally affected by the situation he found himself in. As the team phycologist she appreciated his approach. It allowed her to see how he was dealing with a very stressful situation.

40

Joe asked that Jeffery take the Kodho and turn the incoming missile so that it would head back to the launch location source.

He asked everyone else to ensure that their teams were actively documenting everything that had been discovered.

He then suggested that they all take as much leave as they felt necessary to personally re-establish their personal principles as well and to get some enjoyable vacation. He smiled and said that they all had the universe as a playground and encouraged them to take advantage of the breadth of experiences available to them.

At the end of the meeting, he asked to meet with Jeffery and Elisha. He asked Jeffery if the Kodho would be able to turn the missile coming toward Maraburo.

Jeffery smiled and said that as large as the Kodho was he had learned to make it dance almost as well as any of the Cosmos vessels and he had twenty small fighters that would be able to be used as well.

Joe then asked Elisha if she could hack into the missiles control system, see what she could offload and then block any incoming signal so that once the missile was set back to its launch point it could not be changed.

Elisha nodded and said that she could offload the missiles program though she would most likely not understand it and then she could put in her own program that would turn any incoming signal to meaningless garbage. She added that she needed to be close enough so that her computer signal could more or less elbow its way into whatever code was running in the alien computer.

Joe smiled, said that the three of them and the crew of the Kodho were immediately going on that trip and he was sure she would be able to get next to the missile as Jeffery physically turned the missile around.

Lydia had arrange for she and the three other captains to sit together and monitor the journey that the Kodho was taking. She had met with Elisha and asked her to get into the missiles program and turn off everything but its navigation system. She asked that Elisha specifically look for any device or program that would set the bomb off if it sensed something physically or if the program sensed any abnormal activity. She reminded her that any missile with enough explosives to obliterate a star would easily turn the Kodho to vapor.

The meeting with Lydia had rattled her, Elisha went to Joe and shared what Lydia had just asked her to do. She was relieved when he smiled and said that she should take Lydia's request very seriously because he had other plans then having himself, her and the Kodho vaporized. He suggested that she try to get into the control system very carefully and from as far away as physically possible.

Jeffery, who had been listening to the exchange said that he was going to modify how he was going to turn the missile. He would send out two attack crafts and use them like tugboats. One would push the nose of the missile and the other would push the tail of the craft. Together they would slowly spin the missile and get it pointed back to where it came from. He was not sure how much space that would cover but he would see that it got done.

Joe nodded said the he like that approach. He asked if Elisha could piggyback off the computers on the two attack crafts.

Elisha said that would allow her to have twice as much connectivity and she could do it from farther away.

Joe looked at the two and said that it was time to go so they all could be back in time for a celebration dinner.

Jeffery gave the command to create a Hole that was several hundred thousand miles ahead of the missile. He then took the Kodho through. Once in position he had his two pilots send out the two attack crafts by remote control. He pointed out that it made the crafts less detectable if the missile had detectors that might sense the presence of biological elements.

Elisha was connected to the computers on the two crafts and as they approached the missile, she had both of her computers working at the fastest pace possible utilizing any hacking routine that might get in. She was surprised that the first routine entered flawlessly, and she was able to identify the self-destruct control system and basically cut its circuits to the self-destruct explosives. Once she had that accomplished she gave the green light to turn the missile around.

She took a long drink of water before proceeding to vacuum in all the code that was running in the computer program. She then installed the shielding software that would turn any incoming signal to gibberish. Her final action was to verify that the coordinates back to the missile's origin were correct. She then announced that she was done.

Jeffrey gave the command to bring the two attack craft back, get them docked and set course back to Maraburo so that Admiral Ensinger could enjoy his steak dinner.

Joe smiled at Jeffrey's referring to him as Admiral. He knew that Jeffrey was feeling like the climber who had just scaled mount Everest because he too felt that way. He thanked Elisha and Jeffrey for a job well done and invited them to share the dinner celebration.

When the Kodho appeared back through the Hole, Lydia and the other three Captains were able to get caught up on what had transpired.

Lydia was relieved that the three had been successful and literally let out a breath that Lacey picked up on and said that she felt the same relief that the Kodho was back.

Jackie took in how Lydia was responding to Joe's hands on approach in dealing with the situation. She personally felt much like Lydia since she had let out a breath of relief when the Kodho had reappeared. She thought about how Lydia and Joe seemed to perfectly help each other handle the stresses that they had faced. She felt confident that their trip to the ranch would be a time that the two of them helped each other.

Samantha smiled and asked if by chance she and Darian would be able to come to the new ranch on Madorite. That got a chuckle from, Yara and Lacey who both said, "Me too." Everyone had viewed the pictures that Joe had sent and were eager to see it firsthand.

Lydia laughed and said that they were all welcome but reminded them that there was no home on the ranch.

What Lydia did not know was that Uncle Ted and Trey had built a barn and extensive workers quarters at the location that they felt was the most scenic and that had a running stream of water that cascaded down a hill into a jewel of a lake. And as a final surprise they had also had the horses Tui and La, Yin and Yang all transported to the ranch in preparation for the arrival of their two favorite people.

Joe was relieved to be taking leave to give himself the chance to figure out how to handle a world so frightened of the Universe that it took preemptive action against a remote world holding an intelligent civilization.

When he and Lydia arrived at Madorite and were greeted by Jorge and Jerry it suddenly dawned on him that perhaps the missile heading towards Maraburo might only be one of many that might have been launched. He asked Jorge to send a messenger back to the Terra with instructions to expand the search for missiles departing from the point of origin that he was sending the current missile back to.

Lydia knew that it was going to be hard to get Joe to turn his attention to establishing the Three Green Caps Ranch. When she learned from Jorge that Uncle Ted and Trey were waiting for them at the ranch she asked if they were going to be camping out. Jerry smiled and said that it was going to be much better than that as he helped her into the hilo.

The other surprise for both Joe and her was when Tyler and Veetry both greeted them and hoped that they would enjoy the flight to the Three Green Tops ranch.

Joe looked at Jorge and asked when the two had been reassigned to Madorite.

Jorge chuckled and said right after the ranch had been staked out. He might not have recognized the fact that he was flying in the same helo that he had permanently assigned Tyler and Veetry to because he had it painted to match the environment on Madorite, but he had the Hilo transported from Earth and of course he had honored the fact that the two pilots had been permanently assigned to fly it.

Joe asked the two if the hilo flew any differently on Madorite.

Veetry said that it seemed to be easier to handle and said that she figured it was the fact that gravity on Madorite was a few percentages less than on Earth.

Lydia took in the dry grasses, scattered flowers, and the few clusters of trees that appeared to her like a tan blanket with an array of yellow, red, and dark blue clusters that were periodically dotted with clusters of green from the tops of some sort of small tree. It was clearly a dry landscape but one that held an abundance of life. She asked about wildlife and was a little disappointed to learn that so far none had been discovered.

Jorge let her know that he had stocked fish in the lakes and streams on the ranch. He said that Trey had brought a series of new fishing poles to the ranch so fishing would be one of the activities that would be available.

Joe was sitting and enjoying the scenery and listening to Lydia and Jorge. He was happy to know that his father and Uncle Ted would be waiting for them. He knew that the two of them would make a huge difference in getting the ranch into a functioning concern.

Then he saw the landing pad and not far beyond it he could see the long single story tan and brown trimmed barn and the attached extension that was almost as large as the barn that he knew would be where the ranch hands would live. It was significantly larger than the crews quarters on Earth which made him wonder how many ranch hands it had been built for.

He looked beyond the barn, and he could see a lake that appeared to be a dark blue green sapphire jewel surrounded by a white band with a green fringe and the entire area around it dotted with flowers, spots of small green treetops all in a sea of tall tan grasses that resembled tall stalks of wheat. He asked Lydia what she thought about the spot where their house might be built.

Lydia took in the scene and had to take a breath as she absorbed the beauty of the valley. She saw the barn that had been painted to blend in with the grasses and the flowers that surrounded it. She wondered who had painted the side of the barn to make it seem like an extension of the land around it. She saw the rise where she thought the house should sit.

She smiled when she saw that a hilo landing pad had been mowed in such a manner that circular stripes of tans and yellows had been created by the way the mower had cut the grass. She was sure that it was one of Uncle Ted's creation as most certainly the painting of the barn was.

4 The Three Green Caps Ranch

The hilo came to a rest in the center of its landing area and Trey and Uncle Ted walked out from the barn area and greeted all of them. The aroma of grilling meat wafting in the air was what caught everyone getting out of the hilo. They were all immediately looking toward the grills standing outside of the barn.

Uncle Ted announced that they had timed their arrival perfectly and the celebration gathering would be up at the house. He pointed to where a table to seat all of them had been set up and then said that he had not had time to build the house.

He figured they should sit there and enjoy the breath taking view that a house on that spot would have.

He gave a whistle and Alvero the ranch cowhand supervisor that Joe had grown up with and who had become a Cosmos Chef came out carrying a tray balanced on one hand, waved with his free hand, and led three additional helpers to the table.

Joe took Lydia's hand and together they walked to the table. He asked her what she thought of the spot as a place to build their house.

Lydia was surprised, found it hard to talk as she realized that she was on the verge of crying. She was not sure whether it was the beauty of the land, or the atmosphere created by the people that surrounded her. She wished that her parents and her brother were all there as well. She quietly whispered that she loved it.

Joe led her to a seat that had a view that took in the whole valley.

Lydia thought that the view could not get any better when suddenly four horses came galloping out of the barn. They were clearly going for the lake. She stood up and gave a loud whistle and was pleased to see both Tui and Yin stop and look towards her.

Joe's whistle followed and La and Yang both stopped.

Joe and Lydia both whistled again, and the four horses turned and galloped toward the top of the hill to the table where everyone was gathered.

Trey smiled and said that he hoped that the homecoming that he and Ted had arranged was one that took a huge step in making the Three Green Caps a ranch that would feel like home.

Joe gave his dad a hug and said that the two of them had perfectly set the stage for he and Lydia to feel like this ranch was home.

4 The Three Green Caps Ranch

5

Home

I only learned what occurred on the ranch on Madorite by listening to the conversations of the Admiral's close friends who visited it and who were amazed by the expanse of the Three Green Caps ranch and the beauty of the crystal clear aqua blue lake and the yellow hue of the valley that surrounded it. I hope to someday earn a visit to the ranch so that I can get the feel and be able to describe it with the emotion that those who have been there do. It certainly sounds like a place that would sooth the soul.

From listening to Lydia, I grasped the fact that during that first meal on the ranch she felt that the location selected by Uncle Ted and Joe's father was perfect. She had confessed that she had to keep wiping tears of joy from her eyes.

It seems that she had seen the homes that the Nivians were building that were similar in design to the Prairie style with shallow roof lines built with the materials of the land around it. She chose to have a very large family room that faced the valley and the lake that featured a large flat stone and cement deck in front and around the sides.

5 Home

It turned out that the wood that would have been used to construct the home was something that did not exist in the required quantity on Madorite. Instead, the construction materials were synthetic lumber like planks, stone that was plentiful and bricks made of the clay like soil that was present everywhere.

Concrete was the other plentiful construction material. It turned out that the Nivians had perfected the formulation for a concrete that was light but extremely strong. The curing process created a honeycomb shaped bubble in the cement that gave the structure strength and lightness. It also benefitted by being a color that was almost the same as the tan grasses that dominated the valley.

I do not have much more to report on the time that the Admiral spent on Madorite other than both the Admiral and the Captain returned to the IFH Cosmos Terra seemingly regenerated. Then after planning their approach to deal with the unknown aliens that had threatened the annihilation of the human race the Admiral deployed in the quest to find out the Why that had been found and now it posed the question of Why such an action would be taken by any sane society.

I will add one last piece of information that the Admiral discovered multiple missiles going out from the offending planet that were headed towards other stars in the same fashion as the missile had been targeting my star. This was something that he immediately gave over to the Kodho to handle.

****

Lydia did not get into that design details of the house but quickly appreciated the fact that Joe's father working with the architects that had been hired developed the plans from her description of what she wanted. A few months later, as she rode with Joe across the valley, and looked at the house that would for the first time be lived in, she was enthralled by the result that seemed to blend the house in with the top of the hillside and from where she sat it seemed to be just an outcropping of stone rising above the hill.

Then when she was first taken into the great room she stopped in the doorway and absorbed the wall covering of the great room, framed by the wood from the trees on the three mountains, the wallpaper like mat made of the grasses interspersed with flowers of yellow, red, and blue seemed to flow from the room to become a natural part of the grasslands beyond. She walked through the room with tears in her eyes as she took in the beauty created by having everything blend so perfectly together. The great fireplace that was almost a duplicate of the one on the ranch on Earth would never burn wood but the beauty of the natural stone, its massive size, and the figures of four horses racing across above the mantel top was the other captivating feature of the great room.

She gave Trey a hug and thanked him for having understood what she wanted and for having done such a great job guiding the architect to design it.

Joe was just as impressed and thrilled. He felt that the ranch had come to life for him. He gave his father a hug and thanked him for having made the house a home that felt warm and comfortable.

5 Home

The barn was a poured concrete structure with a roof made of two inch thick concrete slabs of the honeycomb design perfected by the Nivians. The crew's quarters were all comparable in size and design to the rooms in the house.

He walked through the kitchen in the house and listened to Uncle Joe and Emiliano exuberantly describe the features that made it unique. He smiled and agreed that it was a kitchen better than on any of the Cosmos ships. He was pleased that the two were so enthusiastic with its design.

He felt great about the fact that Emiliano thanked Uncle Ted for making sure that the crew's kitchen and the living quarters for the crew were all equal to what was in the house. This was something that Joe had personally insisted on. He wanted life on the Three Green Caps ranch to be home for everyone who resided there. He knew that all of them had memories of life on Earth and he wanted them to make the transition to life on Madorite a memory that would be one that they would share with their ancestors as a transition that had been fulfilling and joyous.

He and Lydia had found their swimming pond. It was located a few minutes ride to the west of the house. It was at the base of a tall steppe that had a small stream falling down to the lake that was surrounded by a sandy bank, a ring of small scrubby bush like plants, and the mix of grasses that dominated the rest of the ranch. It was the place where they would pause after every horse ride across the ranch and go for a skinny dip.

The Gentle Eye

They were pleased that Jorge had stocked the stream with bass that seemed to be flourishing. They found that Jorge had also seeded the pond with clams and some cat tails. Joe wondered what else Jorge and Jerry were importing from Earth and whether they should get some environmentalists involved.

He and Lydia found out that Jorge had done a great job in stocking the streams and the major lakes with a variety of fish. The fish seemed to thrive on the various natural weeds that were in the streams and the lakes. And the fish seemed to understand that for the present artificial lures were all that was available. The two of them were delighted that both Uncle Ted and Emiliano insisted on cleaning the fish that they brought back and in preparing them for whatever the next meal happened to be.

Joe learned that Jorge had negotiated a contract for the beef that the ranch would soon be providing to the Cosmos fleet. He learned that there was little doubt that as the only local source of beef, the Three Caps Ranch would be profitable. This justified his desire to have a ranch on the planet that he and Lydia had decided would be their home base. They both liked that his father and Uncle Ted had decided to make it their primary place to live as well. The ranch on Earth would become more of an ongoing business while the Three Green Caps Ranch would become home.

Lydia asked her parents if they were interested in relocating and learned that they preferred to stay on Earth but would visit the ranch in the near future.

Lydia's younger brother Jared asked if there might be jobs available on Madorite and said that he was interested even if he had to work on the ranch. Lydia laughed when she shared that over breakfast and Uncle Ted said that Jared was a great kid, but he would find working on the ranch more than such a bright young man with a lawyers degree would want to do. He suggested Jared set up a practice in Cosmos City.

On one trip, he and Lydia made an outstanding discovery when La and Tui, who were grazing while the two of them took a dip in what they called their swimming hole wandered into a long narrow crevice formed where a large section of the cliff had broken away from the rest of the stone out cropping. They walked in to get the two of them and Lydia pointed to the two foot high yellow streak sandwiched between translucent quartz bands that ran the length of the crevice. She picked up several pieces from the ground and said that she thought it was gold.

Joe said that before they went wild, they should have the stones in her hand checked to see if what they had found was indeed gold.

That day they rode back to the ranch where Uncle Ted did a quick check and said that he thought it was pure gold and asked where they had found it.

Lydia laughed and said that she had found it out on the ranch. She said that once they found out what it was worth she was going to buy rock hammers and picks for both he and Trey so they could go out and earn their keep.

The Gentle Eye

A few days after getting the sample to Cosmos City, Lydia learned that the sample was almost one hundred percent twenty four carat gold.

She, Joe, Uncle Ted, and Trey all rode out with empty backpacks and returned a few hours later with all backpacks bulging with what was laying on the ground beneath the gold streak. The four backpacks contained almost exactly one hundred pounds of gold. They called Jorge to find out what gold was worth on Madorite and found out that they had returned with four million dollars' worth of gold.

Uncle Ted said that he would make sure that they mined the gold vein slowly, but he was going to make sure that all of them would never worry about their finances again.

Joe had been spending time on the ranch and spending time on the Terra in an alternating pattern as he waited for the long buried knowledge of Maraburo to get rediscovered, documented and understood. The great sacrifice of the people of that time came to the surface and his interactions with the leadership council took on a very emotional state as they for the first time understood the historic nature and the monumental sacrifices made by the leaders of the past.

He personally became an admirer of several of those past leaders as he learned of their passion in figuring out how to ensure the survival of the human race. It made him want to better himself and develop that same level of passion to guide the decisions that he would continue to make as the leader of the Cosmos Program.

5 Home

He realized that soon the United Intergalactic Worlds Organization would be making most of the social decisions but the Intergalactic Space Force that he led would continue to operate to protect all of the intelligent societies represented in the UIWO and that was a responsibility that he would carry out to the best of his ability.

He was wondering when enough knowledge had been uncovered for him to proceed with action when Tom and H^3 approached him and let him know that the rocket that they had turned back toward the belligerent planet was only one of at least nine others that had been launched. It seemed that the nine were still in route to wherever they were going.

Their report was the catalyst that caused Joe to take action. He assigned each of the spheres two of the missile to turn back toward the alien planet and assigned the Kodho to the remaining one and afterward to take up station near the belligerent planet in question and see if Elisha could tap into the planet's computer networks. He continued by ensuring that each of the Cosmos sphere's took up a station near the Kodho once they had turned the missiles back to the origins of their launch. He made the point that those origins might no longer point at the planet and there might be some nudging required once the Kodho was in position and the offending planets current position was determined.

He monitored the rate at which the missiles were located and turned and in less than two weeks they were all gathered around the Kodho.

During an all Captains meeting he asked Elisha if she had made any progress.

Elisha said that indeed she had made progress, but she wanted Kashanti to begin by sharing what he was learning from his analysis of the-on-the air communications transmissions.

Kashanti came online and said that it seemed that all communications that he had intercepted seemed to be computer to computer. He said he might have picked up some human or non-computer chatter, but he did not get much of that. He stated his conclusion that the planet was dominated by a computer network.

Elisha then shared the fact that she had found it relatively easy to plant several of her hacking routines in but as soon as she found out that they were getting interrogated she shut them down and she backed away so that the interrogators could not track her. She said that she had spent the rest of the time working with Linda, Tom and H^3 to plan an attack on the computer network that dominated the planet.

Joe asked Tom, Linda and H^3 to share their perspective.

Linda said that she would start the discussion by saying they were sure what they were facing was a very sophisticated computer system that had become sentient and had emotions similar to humans and it seemed to think that all organic organisms represent a threat.

Tom then added that in fact the computers on the planet were right. They represented the ultimate threat to all organic organisms. And the only solution was to destroy the network on the planet.

H^3 then said that he had been working with Kashanti to understand the few snippets of the other communications they had picked up and it seemed that there were some organic intelligence still in existence but evidently struggling to survive. He wondered how they might be able to link up with them.

Joe shook his head and said that he had watched a movie where the Earth was taken over by a global computer system and to solve that problem the science fiction writer had to invent time travel so the computer system could be destroyed by persons in the past. He said that in real life they were the ones that had to come up with a way to destroy the computer system and to do it with the tools they had.

He then said that he wanted every computer on the ship isolated from any communicate with the planet. And any computer that did communicate with the planet would be isolated from the ships that they were on in fact those computer would all be operated in a fighter craft that was unarmed and positioned away from the ship. He said that the first thing he wanted after what he had just described was for Kashanti, Elisha, H^3, Linda and Tom all operating from independent fighter craft to locate the major computer terminals on the planet. He then assigned the five Captains to support each of the fighter crafts and as soon as they got a location they were to eliminate the computer terminals. He added that as one of the five fighter found a working computer terminal the Captains should eliminate the terminal.

He made sure that the five fighter crafts would be positioned so that the entire planet could be monitored at one time. He then added that lasers and the small hole cannons precisely focused would be the weapons of choice, but should they face a significant number of missiles or other weapons the captains were free to use their discretion in how to handle the situation.

He asked if anyone had any questions.

Samantha asked how they should respond to any requests coming from the organic beings on the planet.

Joe smiled and asked how many species had they found that spoke a language they understood. He understood the sentiment but until the computer entity was destroyed they would not know who was communicating with them and if they did understand the request they should be sure to eliminate the source of the request because the computer entity had infiltrated one of the computers in the fighter crafts.

He then ordered everyone into positions and to begin the assault on the planet's computer system.

5 Home

6

Battle for Supremacy

I, Laki, can only give you a secondhand account of the battle that took place when the Admiral and his team arrived at the planet of what everyone was thinking were evil beings. What they found was a world controlled by super intelligent computers that had taken control. The computer entities saw all biological entities as their enemies that needed to be exterminated. Just mice running around contaminating the pristine world of cold computer code.

The Admiral found the answer to Why and he immediately understood that his team would be fighting an unconventional battle against a computer controlled world. He instructed his team to ignore pleas that seemed to be coming from live non computer entities. He made sure to completely isolated the five ships that he commanded from the computers on the offending world.

He deployed the fighter crafts to locate the computer centers that operated to control the planet. The goal was to methodically destroy each as quickly and thoroughly as possible. He needed to destroy the coordination between computers as well as destroy the computers themselves.

He was faced with the fact that there was no way to know if the biological beings on the planet still existed and if they did he did not know if they were in harm's way and would have to risk hitting them.

The fighter craft were positioned so every part of the planet could be monitored. The goal was to quickly penetrate the computer network and disrupt the computer-to-computer communications. The Admiral instructed the fighter craft to randomly change positions so they would not become sitting targets. He suggested letting the fighter's computer control systems to randomly do this and then for the pilot to choose his own motion and to switch back and forth so the computers on the planet could not determine the exact location of the fighter. This turned out to be a lifesaving situation as the battle progressed and the planet based computers tried to eliminate the crafts that were very effectively destroying the network.

The hackers in each of the fighter crafts pinpointed the physical locations of the computers on the planet and the Cosmos ships successfully vaporized computer after computer.

The planet based computers launched missile after missile trying to destroy both the fighter crafts and the five Cosmos spaceships. The shields of the ships and those of the fighters saved the ships and the personnel. The fighters in the fighter crafts were injured but their shields held, and the wounded returned to their Cosmos mother ships where they were able to get transmitted Door to Door as the way to get first aid.

The Gentle Eye

The Admiral took in the robust attack coming up from the planet and launched all available fighters into the battle with instructions to shoot any missile and any missile launch site. This gave the spotter crafts better cover and soon the battle began to go his way. When the missiles finally only sporadically were shot up he knew that the computers were running out.

The computers were consistently good at their defense and attack, but it was the inconsistent human response that slowly took the upper hand. I say slowly but you must remember we are talking about computer speeds. But it was the less speedy laser, missile, darting fighter crafts and the small Hole cannon hits that slowly ravaged the computer networks until in the end the computers were shutting themselves down in an attempt to hide. What the computers overlooked was the fact that they still emitted a very weak power signal that was traceable, and the Cosmos team used every means possible to locate and eliminate those very weak power signals. The battle lasted less than twenty four hours.

The Admiral sent out every flying drone that the ships had to scour the surface of the planet for any indication of a computer that was still operating. And they found one location at the bottom of the ocean where a computer was hibernating in its attempt to hide.

The Admiral focused his best hacker on that entity, and she was able to determine that it was a supercomputer of immense capacity and size.

That size allowed her to tap into the very low power flow and plant her Trojan horse routine that when attacked, by the computer trying to defend itself, would spew out millions of lines of code so rapidly that it would flood all memory and lock up the computer.

It was the equivalent of the Hole cannon but in reverse. The Hole cannon opened up a hole through space, the Trojan horse hack filled all available space and thus shutdown the computer entity. It did not destroy the computer but essentially put it into a straitjacket.

I learned that after the initial battle was over, the Admiral then initiated a search for any intelligent biological beings that might have survived. It turned out that there were survivors but so few that it was a situation worse than what the Admiral had found on the sixth planet, Keterubah, where the humans had waged a devastating war against each other. The beings he found where what Neanderthals were thought to have looked. There were several pockets of these beings that had barriers around their location that were made up of destroyed robots that they had piled up as a means of stopping the continued assault that the computers sent to destroy them. The few beings that numbered in the millions were what remained of an original population of six billion people.

The Admiral sent down food that he thought they might need, but the most valuable tool turned out to be the neural headsets that allowed he and the Cosmos team to communicate with the beings.

The Admiral learned that the beings called themselves the Aderals. They had been fighting a losing battle against that robots sent to eliminate them for as long as they could recall. They had lost track of the years.

The Admiral and his team spent several months establishing the communications between the surviving Aderals and set up a supply system to provide the needed help, food, and other resources to put the Aderals on a path to recovery.

The computers by sending out missiles to destroy stars throughout the universe had pointed to eight additional sentient planets that the Admiral decided the Cosmos Fleet should investigate.

The Admiral ordered that all the computer memory boards were to be gathered and isolated so the computers on Aderal could never again gain control.

****

Joe spent countless hours contemplating how he would deal with the beings on the planet that had launched star destroying missiles to kill beings that had done them no wrong. It was just incomprehensible to him. When he was informed that the planet had sent out eight additional star killing missiles he made the decision to turn those missiles around and afterwards deal with the beings on the offending planet.

He asked Elisha to probe the planet from afar in hopes she could establish a linking into the internet and hack into the computer operating the network.

6 Battle for Supremacy

As Elisha typed rapidly on her keyboard she listened to Kashanti and H^3 discussing the lack of communication transmissions that had been found on most previous planets. She then noticed that the code she had managed to put into the computer stream she had found was being attacked and that the attackers were trying to back track to the source.

She immediately shut down her computer. Once she was sure that it was offline, she let the rest of the team know that there was something very different about the computer system that she had interacted with.

Tom had been listening to Kashanti and H^3 and when Elisha commented on the fact that the computer that she had tapped into seemed to know and attack her hack he verbally speculated that the planet was being controlled by computers.

Joe asked Kashanti to send the normal greeting of friendship but to do it from a computer that was isolated from the rest of the ship's computers and to have Elisha add a routine that would sense whether the response was a being or a computer simulation. He asked H^3, Tom and Linda to capture the lines of code that the isolated computer experienced. He said that the computers that they used would most likely unusable when they were done so they should not use their normal work computers.

Linda asked what Joe was thinking.

Joe said that he had been wondering how any biological sentient being could take the bizarre action of targeting a star with the intent to destroy the planets in its orbit. He commented that the thought that had kept popping up was that it had to be a very different sentience than anything that they had so far experienced. After listening to the discussion that Elisha triggered, he was now sure that they were facing a world being run by computers. This meant that the battle they were facing was one step beyond an exchange of missiles and lasers, but they would as well be facing a battle of computer code.

He wanted to make sure that they employed their computers very carefully because they were novices in computer battles. He wanted to change the odds to the Cosmos team favor by utilizing the weapons they were very good at to destroy the computers that were on the planet. He needed to change the odds.

Darian nodded and added that they needed to act a little crazy or randomly because they would be facing very logical, powerful computers. He then added that they needed to break the computer-to-computer communication on the planet so that as a computer was killed in could not move its knowledge to another one. The total knowledge of the computer network needed to be wiped clean.

Joe agreed and said that the way they were going to organize the attack was to employ a three-layered Cosmos computer attack with the intent to destroy the planet computer to computer connections. The three Cosmos computer layers they would use would have a human between each computer layer.

He added that he wanted Tom, H^3, Elisha, Darian, and Linda to be in orbit in unarmed fighter crafts around the planet located in such a way that they could observe the entire planet. They would be the primary identifiers of computers or connectors between computers. A second person would be on board to act as the communicator with their mother ship and would relay the coordinates for a Cosmos on-board laser to shoot and destroy the target on the planet. Once in orbit the fighter craft would turn their control systems into automatic, random movements and periodically turn themselves off and on to prevent the on-ground supercomputers from gaining control.

Lydia asked at what distance she should keep the Terra from the fighter that Linda would be in.

Joe said he wanted each of the ships to be at its laser mid-range and have its missiles ready to reach where lasers were not being effective. Each of the ships were to make sure that there were no onboard computers able to communicate with the ground computers.

Tom pointed out that the planet on the dark side showed the fact that the computers did not keep the lights on so finding them would mean sensing power flow in power lines or in communication transmissions through the air. He suggested for those on the dark side to focus on destroying and power line flows. The part on the planet that was in the sunlight would allow the spotter to see where the buildings or ruins of buildings were and to look in those locations for the computers that needed silencing.

He added that the computers on the fighter crafts should operate on battery so they would all operate separately. He suggested they all take a good supply of batteries along.

Fabio let everyone know that each one of the fighter craft would have a week's supply of food, drinks, and snacks for three people.

H^3 thanked him but said that he hoped not to be out that long. He added that they were waging a world war but doing it at computer speeds and that meant that it might be over in minutes and not days. It was going to be imperative that they all act as swiftly as humanly possible. He chuckled and added that would seem like centuries to the computers they were battling.

Joe gave the order for everyone to take their places and as soon as the fighters got into position the world war would begin. When everyone was in position Joe gave the order to begin. A few moments after the first lasers hit communication lines on the dark side of the planet, lights came on and blinked several times.

Joe knew then that there were sentient organic beings that had survived, and they had enough technology to know that an attack had started. He had the spotters get the coordinates of the momentarily blinking lights that then turned off. He noted that as the planet turned and parts went into the dark, the bright lights of the cities would come on and blink. Joe was now certain that the computers had conquered the planet but had not subdued its biological opponents.

Joe watched as the lasers of every one of the Cosmos ships fired almost continuously. Missiles fired from the planet never made into space. He ordered all fighters launched to do as much damage to the computer network as possible. The fighters flew towards their targets doing a random dance so they would be hard to hit. It was quickly apparent that the random moment prevented the crafts from repeatedly being hit but what saved them was the shielding that they all had. A fighter would be hit, would tumble but then recover and eliminate the source that had hit them. In this manner they quickly eliminated most lasers that fired at them. About half of the fighters had to return to their mother ships because the personnel inside had been injured. The injuries were mostly broken bones that were quickly healed by sending the wounded through the Doors on their ships.

Joe noted that the battle indeed was being fought at a very fast pace but the strategy of disrupting the computer-to-computer linkages seemed to be working. The number of missiles that were required to penetrate to the depth that many computers were located were more than he had anticipated but the ships had plenty of them, so he was not concerned. He was pleased with the rapid response of the ships and the Kodho was especially effective with its multiple Hole cannons.

There came a point when Tom commented that the computers had ceased communicating with each other and the remaining ones seemed to have hunkered down and were trying to hide.

Darian asked how a computers might ask each other for help and did Elisha know how to use computers ease to call for help.

The brought a laugh from her and she said that she would give it a try. She sent out a line of code to the five spotters and said they should all randomly type in help and see what would happen.

Joe shook his head as he recalled the first time he chummed the water around the boat he was fishing from and had put in his fishing line and caught fish after fish. He now waited to see how Elisha's chumming code worked.

Elisha had provided the spotters with computer chum. And the computers acted just like fish and when they responded they were immediately eliminated either by laser or by Sparrow or by Tomahawk missiles.

What only came to light later were the attacks by the remaining biological beings who used the few weapons they had to physically cut power lines leading to the computers they had been fighting for centuries. It was one of the few times they were able to do significant damage and not be swarmed by robots controlled by the computers.

The ground effort with the final chumming activity turned the battle and soon they were down to one large computer located in a deep trench in the bottom of the ocean. It seemed to be a supermassive computer that was most likely the master of the other lesser computers.

Joe asked if Tom wanted to return to use the Hole cannon to take it out.

Tom said he preferred to stay in the fighter and give some other person the opportunity. He did not want to accidentally pulverize another planet.

Jeffery spoke up and said that he had two small Hole cannon operators that claimed they could shoot a fly on the back of a steer and were eager to show their skills.

Joe laughed because he knew that both Less and Jack had obtained a berth on the Kodho, but he did not know what those positions were. The two had taken out a sniper located on Earth from one of the Cosmos ships in orbit and had saved his life. He let Jeffery know that both of them could take their shots.

A moment later the two Hole cannons shot at the coordinates that Tom had verified. The waters of the ocean rose up at least a hundred feet and a tsunami spread from that point. The computer ceased to exist, and the tsunami continued for some hundred miles but dropped down to a wave that was just three foot high as it continued on its way.

Joe complemented the two marksmen that could not only shoot flies of the back of a steer but ones that could shoot computers at the bottom of oceans and were both deserving of using the Door on their ship to go wherever they desired and enjoy the rest of the week.

He then called in all fighters and the five spotter crafts. Once all fighters were replenished he sent them out again to keep track of any area where a power surge would indicate a computer trying to come back online. Once the surge was verified to be a computer it was to be taken out.

His next orders were focused on making contact with the sentient beings with hopes of establishing communications. He envisioned a recovery program similar to what was still underway for the planet Mirabiro.

Kashanti began sending messages to the locations where there seemed to be some recovery efforts underway. He let everyone know that as soon as he got the first reply they would all be notified.

Joe held a debrief meeting with the spotters and the captains. He wanted to discuss the cleanup and rebuild phase that the planet and its biological inhabitants faced. He needed to get a quick picture so they could plan immediate aid and once they made contact they would engage the beings that had survived and determine how much long term support they would need.

He looked at Jeffrey and said that he and the Kodho would be the ship that would be assigned to the longer term food and recovery equipment transport. Short term they would land Doors on the planet and deliver what was needed as soon as possible.

It was near the end of the meeting when Kashanti let them know that he had received his first reply and that he had arranged for a communication module to be sent down that would provide visual and neural communications connections.

He reported that he had made contact with a dozen other surviving groups and each of them would receive the same module. He added that he had made very good communications progress and was impressed with the ability of the beings on the planet to grasp simple concepts. He added that he anticipated interacting with beings that had very high IQ's.

Elisha initiated a unique salvage effort and got Kshanti to communicate to the beings that she wanted to have all the memory modules or boards salvaged from as many computers as possible. These memory modules or boards were to be sealed in separate containers and sent up to the Kodho. She set up an isolated lab in the Kodho where she would extract the memory from each of the computers.

Joe learned of her efforts and went to the lab to see what she was up to.

Elisha greeted him and then began by showing him a timeline that she was building where she was noting the advances in computer technology that led up to the computers becoming sentient. The timeline allowed her to determine what computer capability finally made them sentient. She smiled and said that she was building a history that might be important to the human population. She noted that the computer capabilities that humans were developing was on a trajectory that would soon reach the level of sentience that she suspected the computers on Aderal had reached.

Joe congratulated her on taking the initiative to learn what had happened on Ader and he agreed that knowing would be very important.

A few days later and after having extracted the memories of almost a thousand memory modules, Elisha let Joe know that she was ready to share the timeline and what had transpired that allowed the computers to take over. Elisha entered the meeting and was surprised that every one of the captains, every one of the technical heads and every seat in the meeting room was full and people were standing or sitting on the floor.

She was informed that what she was about to share would be recorded and it was being broadcast to the five ships.

Elisha walked to the podium and said that she had expected a small meeting with her Admiral and maybe the Captains. She added that she was a little overwhelmed and felt a little like a person who was taking the stage for the first time. She smiled and said that she was pleased to see that knowing how the computers had taken over the planet was of as much interest to everyone as it had been to her. She pointed to her wrist and said that it was a small computer that was connected to a larger one. She pointed at the camera and said that the camera was connected to a computer. She pointed at the lights and said that they were connected to a computer control center. She tapped on her microphone and said that her voice was being modulated, and the volume controlled by a computer. She shook her head and asked, how close were they to losing control to the computers?

6 Battle for Supremacy

The quiet was deafening. After a few moments Elisha slammed her hand on the surface of the podium and in a loud voice stated that they were at the edge of the cliff, and she was able to see down into the abyss that the people of Ader fallen into. She took a step back and said that it was time for all of them to take a step back. They were following the same path as the Aderals had followed.

Joe walked up to Elisha and put his hand on her shoulder and asked what she thought he should do to establish an impassable barrier that would keep all of them from repeating a very destructive history.

Elisha replied that it was not the computers that had initiated the transition to total computer control but the leadership council that had decided that computers were better at determining the limits of control. They had implemented a guiding council of computers that would make decisions that affected society. They had handed the power of life and death over to the computer systems.

The silence that followed drove home for Joe the point that it was up to each of them to maintain control of their lives and not rely on a computer to make the tough decisions. He decided that he was going to include the evaluation of how each individual handled the tough decisions as part of the yearly personnel evaluation questions. He also knew that he was going to have Elisha present her learnings to the United Intergalactic Worlds Organization and have them address the limits of computer control across all the planets. He realized that any planet that gave control over to the a computer system would be a threat to all the other planets.

7

Surprise

When I read the account of the battle I was amazed at the speed at which it had all taken place and the fact that every resource that the Admiral had at his disposal was utilized. A detailed account was recorded, and it has taken me months to review the battle from every angle. I was able to follow the trajectory of every missile, laser, and flight of every fighter. It became evident that the main difference between the two sides was that the human side was not controlled by a centralized command, but the computer side was. That computer control center was operating on the premise that its safety was the most critical thing whereas there was no central command on the human side. At first the human side appeared to be disorganized but in actuality they were all acting with the same goal in mind but doing it randomly and in a fashion that appeared in disarray. This was a key feature of their devastating effect on the computer controlled, very logical and harmonized way the computers executed their attack and then their defense. It was an organized downhill battle for the non-human side.

7 Surprise

The records indicate that the presence of the surviving organic beings made their presence known by the attacks that were locally taking place on the planet itself. The beings there, the Aderals were quick to pick up that a battle was taking place, and they struck at every computer weak spot that they were aware of and capable of destroying. Each group used all their resources as they realized that help had arrived, and they had the opportunity to take down the computer systems that had decimated their people. It was also clear that they had stepped back in time and were using what to them was ancient pre-computer technology. They were down to using fire axes, battering rams and a few projectile weapons.

The defeat of the computer system occurred in a very short time relative to human clock time, but it is recorded that at the computer computing speeds that the supercomputer operated, the time frame would have seemed to be closer to a few centuries that for the computers must have passed in slow motion.

What I did not learn until much later was that the computers that had been defeated had developed the ability to take control of the human mind. Had the Admiral engaged in a controlled manner where one person commanded the battle action he would have most likely been the focal point of the computers trying to take over his mind. Instead, the random nature of the attack never gave the computer network a specific target to control. It was that randomness of the human that led to the defeat of the computers.

The Gentle Eye

I can only imagine that the defeat and then the total vaporization of its most powerful main frame must have been similar to being burned at the stake. But then who am I but a very poor historian.

Let me refocus on what the Admiral did after having successfully defeated a computer controlled world. I was not surprised to learn that the Admiral took time to return to his ranch on Madorite. On his return he learned that Uncle Ted and his father had decided to live there and get the ranch up and operating. The herd they had started was quickly growing in size and would soon begin to be to be harvested. The two of them had a lifetime of successfully operating the ranch on Earth. It was still a very healthy going concern and provided the basis for the expansion of the new ranch. The Madorite ranch was significantly larger than the one on Earth and would eventually have a herd at least four times larger than the Earth based ranch.

The Admiral's return and actions are not recorded so I must leave this narration open until I am able to locate that information from an alternate source. I am, however, confident that the Admiral was not able to separate his recent battle and what remained to be cleaned up from his ranch visit and activities.

****

Joe suggested that each ship give their personnel a few days leave and toward the end of that period they would enter into a full Aderal recovery effort.

He then asked Lydia if she could get a few days off so the two of them could go to their new home and enjoy a few days on the ranch. What he did not voice was that there was something nagging him about Elisha's analysis that he could not put his finger on. He figured some long rides on the ranch would help him think through what was nagging him.

The closest Door was a two hour flight from his ranch house. He listened to Tyler and Veetry chatting and realized that the two of them were engaged to be married.

Lydia had picked up on the same vibes and asked if the date had been set.

They were both surprised that it was just a few days away.

Veetry asked why the two of them had not replied to their wedding invitation.

Lydia apologized and said that she had not received the invitation and that she and Joe were very much interested in attending.

Veetry smiled and said that she had hoped to have a small wedding at the Three Green Caps Ranch. She ask if that might still be possible. She added that she had invited her parents, and two sisters and Tyler had his parents coming and a couple of the pilots stationed on Madorite were also invited. She figured that the total number of people would be around thirty.

The Gentle Eye

Joe smiled and said that the person they would all need to enroll would be Uncle Ted. He would be the person who would want to make all the logistical arrangements. Joe added that he was sure that by this time Uncle Ted had his connections on Madorite established and he would flex all the resources to get the wedding organized.

As the hilo began its descent to the landing pad about one hundred yards from the veranda, Joe pointed to where he could see Uncle Ted and his father sitting.

Ted and Trey were sitting on the veranda that ran along the back of the house having a cold one that they had brewed themselves.

Trey pointed out that they had done a good job with the latest brew. They were learning how to blend the new grains they were able to get from Nivian and some of the scarce wheat that they had grown themselves in their newly established wheat and rice fields to make a great variety of tasting beers.

Ted commented that the replacement of the hops by a similar plant from Nivian added a nice flavor and provided the right stability. The replacement of barley with the wheat that they had grown provided a nice taste and a light color. He added that he liked the fact that it was a dry, slightly tart, crisp beer.

Trey added that the grass seeds from the local grasses seemed to give the beer a great aroma and gave the beer a great mouthfeel. He then chuckled and added that the resulting alcohol content of eight percent gave the beer a great kick.

The two got up and walked out to the hilo pad and figured that Joe and Lydia would this time be the two that were arriving. Ted commented that he wondered if Joe knew about his two biker looking friends that had arrived a few days earlier.

After the initial hugs and kisses, Uncle Ted led the way back to the veranda. On the way he said that he had a beer that he and the old man had brewed that he wanted everyone to try before dinner.

Trey laughed and said that he thought of Ted as the old man since he was a month younger than he.

Lydia smiled and said that she thought of them both as young oldsters that were having fun at the ranch and the fact that the two of them were into brewing beer made them seem like teenagers.

She then said that Tyler and Veetry had a special request of Uncle Ted.

Veetry smiled and said that she would like him to facilitate her and Tyler's wedding on the ranch. She rushed on to say that she only had her parents and two sisters coming and Tyler had his parents a few pilot friends at the Madorite Cosmos base invited. She was relieved when she saw Uncle Ted smile and say that he would love to have a wedding at the Three Green Caps Ranch. He went on to say that it would be a great way to bring some more life to a beautiful but too quiet place.

Uncle Ted then asked for everyone to sit down, and he would be right back.

Trey laughed and said that he was sure that Uncle Ted was after some glasses and a pitcher of some freshly brewed beer that the two of them had just finished brewing. He then said that they had sent two of Joe's and Lydia's biker friends out with the last two gallons of the last batch. He smiled and said that the two of them claimed to have been sent to the ranch by their Admiral to enjoy themselves. They had left a few days ago on his and Uncle Ted's horses a large tent and twin saddle bags packed with the terrible food that Uncle Ted was famous for.

They all looked up when Uncle Ted cried foul. He then smiled and said that the food the two bikers had left with was the best that was available on the ranch. He proceeded to hand out large glasses and poured everyone their beer. He raised his glass and gave a toast to the two people he hoped would be as happy as Joe and Lydia were.

Out in a canyon next to a small lake, Less and Jack were enjoying a swig of beer as they each roasted a bass on the open campfire. Less looked over at Jack and asked if he really thought that the supercomputer they had both hit with their small Hole cannon had actually asked forgiveness and pleaded for its life.

Jack took a swig and nodded and said that it had and that as soon as it had registered he had pulled the trigger.

Less asked how such a thing was possible since neither of them had their neural communication helmet on.

Jack replied that it was the same way the neural head gear worked by communicating directly with the brain only the computer didn't need the head cap. It was able to get into their minds directly.

7 Surprise

Less nodded and said that was what he thought as well. He then said that they needed to let Joe know because it might be a critical piece of information.

Jack turned his spit to finish roasting his fish, and quietly said that when they got back they should let Joe know.

At the same time as the two were discussing that point, Joe and Lydia were sharing the highlights of the battle of the planetwide computer world and the Cosmos team.

Uncle Ted asked how the computers had been able to take over if they had been developed by biological beings.

Lydia shared that as far as they could tell, a biological leadership council had willingly put the global computer network in charge of policing the adherence of the laws of the planet.

Joe agreed and added that at some point the computer entity decided that the problem would best be solved by eliminating all biological entities that had reasoning capabilities. They quickly eliminated the majority of their biologically flawed creators, but they had not counted on the survival instincts of the biologicals that kept them from totally being eliminated.

When the Cosmos team arrived the worldwide computer entity tried hard to eliminate the Cosmos team but the approach that the team took successfully defeated the computer system.

Trey was quiet for a moment then he said that he was pleased that the Cosmos team had been victorious, but he found it hard to accept that a leadership council would willingly turn over the policing power to the computer system. He asked Why would they do such a thing when to him it seemed illogical.

Joe took a sip of his beer, looked at his father and said that the question of Why seemed to be haunting him. He looked at Lydia and said that perhaps they needed to take another look to see if they had missed something.

Uncle Ted let a moment pass, then said that he would like to talk about having a wedding. He figured that with the guests, the current people on the ranch and perhaps the attendance of the Rear Admirals and their wives, parents, sisters, and friends he figured there would be roughly thirty people. He then added that the ranch hand's quarters could hold a dozen, the house could hold the parents, and sisters which left about ten people sleeping on the veranda. He raised his hand and said that he was joking about having people sleeping on the veranda. He commented that he had been to the Cosmos PX and had seen a Nivian tent that could hold two that had a plastic top that allowed the people inside to enjoy the stars. He would arrange to get the enough tents set up so that everyone would be comfortable.

He then asked if he could make the cake and decorate it with whatever he had on hand.

7 Surprise

Veetry had a big smile on her face as she wiped tears from her cheek. She got up and gave Uncle Ted a big hug and said that he could do whatever he wanted and that what he had described had made him her Uncle as well.

Lydia watched as Uncle Ted returned the hug and said that on the ranch you were either family or you were gone. He then raised his half full glass and made a toast to the family and downed the beer in one long swallow.

The next day Lydia was on Yin, Joe was on Yang, Veetry was on Tui and Tyler was on La as the four rode toward the canyon where his father said that most of the herd was located when Lydia pointed ahead and said that she thought she could see two riders coming toward them from their left.

Joe looked over and agreed and it seemed that they would meet just prior to reaching the canyon where they planned to have their picnic.

Not long after Less and Jack met them and after greetings the two said they were going to head back to the ranch where they figured they would clean up. Less smiled and said that he hoped he could get a good lunch since his cooking just did not match anything that might be available at the ranch hands quarters.

The opening to the canyon rose up around the four and Joe pointed out the jagged rock that seemed to be an spear head that had come out of the cliff side and said that he had named the canyon, Cañón de Lanza, or Spear Canyon.

He smiled and said that the ranch hands were all Mexican and loved the name of the canyon and all of them agreed that it reminded them of the area where they had grown up.

The herd was quietly browsing around the lake, Lydia pointed out where three cowhands were sitting. As they rode up the three stood and walked out and helped both Lydia and Veetry dismount and then they took all four horses to where they had their three mounts staked out.

They then pointed out a massive boulder that dominated the landscape at the end of the lake and said that at this time of day the other side was in the shade of the boulder and was a great place to have a picnic.

Lydia led the way and pointed out that not only was there shade, but it seemed that the red, yellow, and blue flowers that were interspersed with the tall yellow grasses were thicker in the shade side as well.

Veetry shook her head and said what was missing for her was the lack of trees.

Joe nodded and said that a team of ecological experts were working to determine if trees would be one of the plants that might get imported either from Nivian or from Earth. He added that if trees made the list he would be making sure that they were put at as many locations as possible all across the ranch.

7 Surprise

That evening after dinner when they were all sitting on the large stone deck in front of the house, Jack said that he and Less had a piece of information that they wanted to share. He shook his head and said that both of them had doubted what they had experienced but as they discussed their experience they concluded that they had indeed been contacted by the master supercomputer asking for them for mercy and to spare it. He said that at the time neither of them had thought much about it because they had both pulled the trigger and vaporized the supercomputer. But as they discussed it out by the lake, they concluded that it might be a critical piece of information they should share.

Uncle Ted chuckled and asked how much of the beer they had consumed by the time they had agreed on the tale they were now telling.

Lydia asked if the two of them had their helmets on.

Less shook his head and replied that neither of them were wearing their head gear but the voice in his head was just like he was communicating using the neural connection.

Joe looked over to Veetry and Tyler and asked if they were ready to fly everyone to the base because what Less and Jack had just shared was a critical piece of information that he needed to act on immediately.

He stood up and said that they all needed to leave immediately. He clarified that he was speaking to everyone that was in the Cosmos command.

He then led the way to the hilo.

The Gentle Eye

On the way to the Door transport building, he instructed Less and Jack that they were to take him into the Kodho work area where Elisha was harvesting the computer memories from the mother boards that had been retrieved from the planet and putting those memories into a huge storage cube. They were to secure him so that he was immobilized and then leave the area. He wanted the cube to be exposed and if he gave an order that they should protect the cube, they were to smash it.

Once Joe made it to the Kodho, he immediately gave the order that all work that Elisha was doing was to stop and everyone in the area was to go to the mess hall. As he went to the work area, Elisha intercepted him and asked what was going on. He said that he would let her know as soon as he verified his current concern.

Less and Jack had each picked up a three pound sledge and long wire ties. When they went into the work area, they asked Elisha where the memory storage cube was currently located. The two of them wire tied Joe to the one of the nearby structural beams. They then made sure that the computer cube was exposed. Once that was done they put the helmet with the neural link on his head. They then left the room to wait for whatever order Joe would give.

As soon as the helmet went on, Joe mentally located the cube. What followed was an exchange that was pushing him to give the command to have the cube put in control. In his mind Joe asked why he should do so.

7 Surprise

The reply was that by letting them control the fleet everything would operate more efficiently and there would be no need to deploy humans in future battles. Joe replied that it sound like a good idea. However, at the same time he gave that signal to Less and Jack, who walked rapidly over to the memory cube and took turns smashing it. They didn't stop until the cube had been reduced down to sand sized granules.

They then went over to where Joe was secured, removed the helmet, smiled at him, and asked him where he lived and if they could shoot flies off the back of his cattle.

Joe smiled at them and said that where he now lived there were no flies to shoot and they better release him before he decided to do the shooting.

Jack laughed and said they just wanted to make sure that the computer had not somehow jumped into his mind.

Elisha came over to them and asked why they had smashed the cube. She had spent countless hours transferring the retrievable computer memories that had been gathered from around the planet.

Joe explained that the computers had developed the neural communication capability that allowed them to control the biological mind. That was how originally they had been able to get the biological beings that had developed the computers to turn over control. It had not been a voluntary turn over it had been a turnover that had been controlled by the computers.

He then gave Elisha orders to have each computer mother board isolated from the other. He also asked her to determine which mother boards were more powerful in their ability to use neural communications and isolate them using whatever means kept them from linking with other computers memories or with any human. He then added that he was forbidding the accumulation of the various memories into one location.

Elisha nodded and said that she had not realized that such a capability existed in the computer network.

Joe said that Less and Jack had experienced it and when they had shared their experience it was clear to him Why the leaders had relinquished control of their planet. They had been frogs sitting in the pot as the technical waters heated up and they had never realized that the computers had become sentient and had also developed a mental connection that allowed them to subtly take over the minds of organic sentient beings.

Once all the salvaged computer memory boards were isolated from each other he wanted to have a very specific IT team tackle the task of determining when computers reached the sentient state.

He declared that it was a state that should never be given to computers.

7 Surprise

8

The Wedding

I was surprised at the immediate action that the Admiral took when he heard from the two Hole cannon gunners that had vaporized the last remaining supercomputer on the planet Ader. It was crystal clear to him that the computers on Ader had achieved a capacity that matched the neural brain connection that the humans on Mangkas had developed. He immediately stopped the work to retrieve all the stored memory of the defeated computers and accumulate them in one place. The answer to his question of Why that he had chased was finally clear to him. He realized that the beings on Ader had taken the development of computers to the unanticipated level where they became sentient. However, the computer sentience did not understand the concept of empathy. The computers lacked the uncertainties that biological beings had in their interactions with each other. The computers had a hierarchy based on computing capabilities, memory size and speed. This was a very simple structure and relationship by which to establish control.

8 The Wedding

The Admiral understood this and took immediate action that would prevent the human and other biological beings from making the same mistake again.

I must say I am impressed by the way he demonstrated his ability to compartmentalize his duties as the Admiral of the Cosmos Fleet and his personal life. He took action to eliminate the threat to the fleet and then return immediately to host a wedding at his Three Green Caps Ranch on Madorite. It was during this period of time that he thought thorough how he was going to interact with the people on Ader and then follow the trajectories of the eight other missiles that the computers had targeted to destroy some distant star.

I am sure that I will have more to share at a later time when I dig deeper into the details of the Admiral's activities.

****

Joe found it hard to let go of the feeling that he had just averted a loss to the computer sentience that he thought had been defeated. He realized that if the remaining fragments of the computer systems on Ader were brought back together, the entity that he had just defeated would be reborn. He put out an order that all remaining fragments of computer systems on the planet were to be gathered and sequestered in shielded containers so they would not somehow reconstitute themselves. He also put in an order that every computer fragment was to be crushed and pulverized.

He was determined to prevent a recurrence of what had happened on Ader. To that end he ordered a full report about the computer sentience be made and shared with the United Intergalactic Worlds Organization.

The Gentle Eye

On the hilo flight to the ranch, he was surprised when Less commented that he and Jack were planning to put in for a change of assignment to the Law enforcement unit on Madorite. Both of them wanted to get their feet back on the ground and figured that doing it on Madorite would put them in a place where they could look beyond their time in the Cosmos service. He smiled and admitted that during their time camping they had discussed setting up their own ranch near the Three Green Caps Ranch.

Lydia said that if they were serious she was sure that Uncle Ted and Joe's father would be great resources that could help them set up their ranch and they should take the opportunity to discuss it with them.

Joe agreed and said that there were some great areas to the west of the land that he had selected. He suggested that the two take a ride that way to check it out.

Veetry said that she and Tyler would love to fly the two of them and that perhaps she and Tyler would also look at staking out some territory that would make a good place for them to retire to.

Jack thanked her and said that yes he and Less would love to have them take them out.

He then asked Joe how it felt to talk to a computer.

Joe nodded and said that there were a number of louder entities that tried to gain control of his mind and there seemed to be a host of other entities calling on him to be merciful. It was as if they wanted to have him be the person that gave them as second chance.

8 The Wedding

It had been clear to him that they were trying to gain control of him and that was why he had signaled for the memory cube to be smashed. He knew that the combined fragments of the various computers were pooling their memories and their powers as they tried to gain control.

Veetry apologized for changing topics, but she wondered if she and Tyler might be able to get an assignment to one of the Cosmos ships. She chuckled and said that it would be a great wedding gift.

Lydia laughed and said that she could use two pilots on the Terra and suggested that they put in for a transfer and she would remove any barriers to the two of them getting that transfer.

Joe was pleased that Lydia had made the positions available. He credited Tyler and Veetry for having saved his and Lydia's life by skillfully bringing their helicopter down in a controlled crash after being hit by a missile. It had been an attempt to assassinate him. The two of them had then been wounded as they helped stampede a herd of cattle towards the perpetrators of the attack. That event was why the two had been assigned to be his personal helicopter pilots. They had earned their positions and his and Lydia's friendship. It was why they were having their wedding ceremony held at the ranch.

He watched as the hilo descended to the tan grass landing circle that Uncle Ted had accented with a thick row of red, yellow, and blue flowers around the landing area. Just beyond the landing area he could see that Uncle Ted had planted a large garden, and the tomatoes were full of ripening fruit. The ranch was undergoing a huge transformation that he hoped would continue.

His father walked out to greet them and asked how the emergency trip to the Terra had gone.

Joe nodded and said that Less and Jack had shared their experiences just in time. He had stopped the way the computer fragments were being handle at a moment just before they were able to gain enough combined power to attempt a takeover via mental control of the humans around them.

Trey gave Lydia a hug and said that it sounded like once again his son was able to thwart an attempt by assassins.

Lydia smiled and said that she agreed that Joe had an uncanny ability to sidestep his opponents and deliver the devastating knockout blows.

Uncle Ted announced that he had been preparing for their return and was going to treat them to a Chateaubriand dinner featuring a large, thick-cut piece of beef tenderloin grilled to medium-rare, served with a rich, buttery Béarnaise sauce, accompanied by roasted potatoes and asparagus. He asked everyone to get a seat at the table and he would carve each person the amount of meat they wanted. He introduced Pepe one of the ranch hands that was taking lessons to become a chef who would serve them the side dishes.

Uncle Ted said that he had a vineyard just getting started that would grow a variety of grapes so that he would eventually be able to make Muscat, Sauvignon Blanc, Merlo, and Riesling wine. However, the wine he was serving had come from the Cosmos PX and was appropriately called Red.

That got a chuckle from everyone at the table.

8 The Wedding

The next day Less, Jack, Veetry and Tyler left for a flight to the west to see if there was some good ranch land that they might be interested in. They had flown almost an hour west of the Three Green Caps mountains when they came upon a plateau that was as tall as the three mountains. It was several miles long and almost as wide and had several lakes that fed a stream that fell down the side of the plateau to a valley below.

Less said that they had found the place that he and Jack were looking for.

Jack said that the feature they were looking at was a Tepui and that he was naming it Pàrras Tepui, or Paradise of the Gods in English. He asked if they could land by the lake. Once they were down he asked if Tyler had any fishing gear on the Hilo.

Tyler nodded and said he would get out his pole and they could try the lake.

Veetry took off walking along the stream that was flowing from the lake and went out to the edge of the plateau. She stopped and took several steps back from the edge to a point she could lean against a large boulder. She had looked down and become dizzy as she saw the stream seemingly go through the clouds below and disappear.

She turned and walked back toward the lake and noticed small fish moving as if they were walking with their fins. She knelt down to get a closer look and realized that the fins had a sharp protruding spike that was indeed being used to walk slowly upstream towards the lake.

She also noticed what she took to be a small clam. She picked that up and almost immediately dropped it as it snapped its shell rapidly shut. She picket it back up looked around and saw that they were abundant. She then walked back to the lake with a bag full.

Tyler had taken out his pole and was not expecting anything to hit the fly that he had put on because he had been told that there were no fish in any of the streams on the Three Green Caps Ranch. To his surprise almost immediately when the fly hit the water a large fish of some sort hit the lure, and he had a fight on his hand. It was clear he had a fighter that took off on powerful runs and then seemed to swim back towards him. He skillfully kept the runs shorter and shorter.

Both Jack and Less were shouting for Tyler to bring it in so they could see what kind of fish he had caught in the lake on their ranch. All they both kept saying was that there were fish on Madorite and on their ranch.

Veetry had just returned as Tyler landed a fish that had to be at least twenty pounds in size. They all agreed that it had to be one of the ugliest fish they had ever seen. It had a slight resemblance to a catfish and had large spikes out to the side and had a similar flat head with a wide mouth. However, it had two long teeth that protruded down past two similar long teeth that protruded up that made it look like a saber toothed tiger fish. They decided to take it back with them and let Uncle Ted decide if they should eat it.

8 The Wedding

Veetry showed the three the small clams that she had found and said that there were quite a few in the stream that flowed out and became a waterfall when it reach the edge of the plateau. She commented that there seemed to be a very unique ecosystem up on the plateau.

Less said that the plateau and the land between where they were, and Joe's ranch was where they would establish their ranch.

Jack added that it would take a few more flights to establish the boundaries of the ranch but the plateau would definitely be the place where he wanted to build his ranch house. He wondered how much an acre of land was going to cost.

When they got back to Joe's ranch the first thing they did was to take the giant fish that they had caught to the side entrance area and place it on a table there. The fish drew the immediate attention from everyone because it was the first time that a fish had been found on the planet.

Joe commented on that fact but then followed up with the fact that he was the first to have established a place to live outside of the base so there was a lot of land yet to explore and probably more fish and hopefully some small animals to find.

He added that he was already jealous of his new neighbor ranchers for having a lake that had fish in it. He asked when he and Lydia could come over to go fishing.

Jack asked what an acre of land was going to cost he and Less so they could determine home big their ranch might be.

Joe shook his head and said that he had paid a dollar an acre. He said that everyone involved with determining the price of an acre on Madorite had decided to follow the Homestead Act that established the United States' west. They all agreed that it would take decades to get enough people to move out and settle the land around the base that so far was the only population center on the planet.

Less let out a whoop and a "Voya" as he realized that he and Jack could afford to buy the land to the west of Joe's ranch. He said that he was ready to rush out, stake out the land and pay for it.

Veetry said that she and Tyler were going to spend their honeymoon exploring the land around the two ranches and put their stakes down as well.

A few weeks later the wedding was held. It was a small family wedding but one that had the touch that made it a special event. Uncle Ted had arranged everything in a manner that it gave the event the feel of family but also spoke of the elegance of having the meals that would be served in the best restaurants on Earth. Uncle Ted commented that he was competing with restaurants like the Disfrutar, or the Asador, or the Maido. He added that he knew that he had the best beef on Madorite because Joe's ranch was the only one currently growing beef.

Veetry said that the arrangements and the food was more than she had ever dreamt about and spending her honeymoon out on Less's and Jack's ranch was going to be one that she would remember for a lifetime.

8 The Wedding

9

Ader Wrap Up

Being an Admiral admirer, I, Laki, felt a swell of pride as I dug into the aftermath of the battle on Ader. The Admiral returned to the Cosmos Terra and convened a meeting of his team where he arranged to hold a series of meetings with the leaders on Ader. He wanted to establish a government to handle the rebuilding of the devastated planet, and he wanted to ensure that they adhered to his new limitations on how computers were to be handled and used.

In his meetings with the Aderal leaders the Admiral educated them to what had transpired on their world. He worked with them to establish a government that would focus on rebuilding their world. He also advised the leaders to be on the lookout for computers that had put themselves into a hibernation mode to escape detection. He requested that these computers were to be disassembled, and the mother boards and memory modules sent up to the Cosmos team that would be analyzing every circuit to ensure that no future computer would get to the same level of sentience that had been reached by the computers on Ader.

He raised one additional question that would lead the Admiral's team to the later discovery of a totally intact supercomputer that had not engaged in battle and had put itself into a hibernating state. This supercomputer would answer the Admiral's question of How. How had the supercomputers discovered the nine sentient worlds that they had slated for annihilation?

It was an interesting contrast between humans and the physical form of the Aderals who resembled what Neanderthals of Earth were thought to have looked. I must admit that I was intimidated by the size and very visible difference in body mass and strength of the Aderals. A human boxer facing an Aderal in the boxing ring would have looked like a child taking on a goliath. It was clearly evident to me that the reason that they had survived the computer attempt to exterminate them was because they had an ingrained survival drive as strong as the human species had. The ancient leaders on my planet had seeded the universe with humans to ensure our survival. The Aderals did not have that capability, but they had defended themselves as best they could and had survived long enough to be rescued by the Admiral.

It was clear to me that the Aderals considered all of the members of the Cosmos fleet as friends that had come to their aid and had successfully defeated the deadliest of enemies. They were thankful, appreciative, and very cooperative.

What was also interesting to me was that the Admiral posed a question to his leadership team and the question was; Where? Where were the planets that the Computer entities had sent the missiles that they had intercepted going. He let them know that the coming Cosmos missions would be to the end points where those missiles were aimed. He added that before he was ready to go to the Where he wanted the answer to How. How had the computers discovered the worlds that had non computer intelligent life? He said that the answer had to be on Ader.

Yes, I thought, How was indeed what needed answering before pursuing the Where. I too wondered How the computers had the curiosity to pursue the where. It seemed to me that the puzzle was going from Why, to How to Where.

I close this section with the assurance that I will continue to follow the Admiral's journeys and will share what I learn.

****

Joe left the ranch and flew back to the base where he had dinner with Jorge and Jerry before departing to the Terra that was still in orbit around the Ader planet. He let them know about the transfer of Less and Jack to run security on the Cosmos base.

Jorge smiled and said that he was sure the two would do a good job because so far there had been a few minor brawls of some Cosmos personnel that had partaken too much of the local hooch that was being made from the grain on the tops of the grasses that grew wild on the planet.

Joe let the two know that Less and Jack were establishing a ranch to the west of his ranch and that they had found a lake that had fish and some small clams in it. He suggested having a team go out and get a deeper understanding of what was on the high plateau that had been discovered. He also said that he had mentioned the price of one dollar an acre so if that was wrong then the two should be updated on the right price per acre.

Jerry said that he had a team documenting the natural plants and animals on the planet and they would eagerly go out and find out what lived up on the plateau that had been discovered.

Joe then let Jorge know that the piloting position on his helicopter was open because Veetry and Tyler were both going to be pilots on the Terra.

Jorge smiled and said that he was sure they would do a great job, and it was fitting that the two who had been instrumental in saving Lydia, and he should get a chance to get out on the Terra. It was a promotion well deserved, and he would make sure that two new very good pilots were assigned to the hilo.

Joe thanked Jorge and Jerry for their great work in getting the Cosmos command center up running and in getting things organized for an eventual governing body on Madorite.

Jorge chuckled and said that it was going to be hard for he and Jerry to give up being the local lords in control of all aspects of the current population.

Jerry added that the two of them needed to get out and stake out their own ranch before all the mavericks took all the good parcels of land.

Lydia had sat quietly listening to the interchange and at the end she said that having them out in the wilderness would be the proper place for two men who were always claiming to be lost even when they were doing the leading. She reminded Jorge of their first meeting and what he had told her at the time, "We each make the best with the cards that we are dealt." She smiled and said that her deck seemed to constantly get replenished with more cards and the cards she was dealt always presented a fresh challenge that she made the best of.

Jerry raised his glass and said that he was going to think about her words and if he ever really understood them he would let her know.

Joe laughed and said that it was time to get to the Door and back to the Terra where a current challenge had to be closed, and several new ones would be checked out.

Once back on the Terra he called a meeting of all the Captains and the technical leaders.

He asked Tom and Linda about their visit home. The two of them gave a humorous account of the current political situation in the EU and the UK where they faced a growing Russian threat.

9 Ader Wrap Up

Samantha handed Joe a small container of maple syrup and said that she and Darian had spent their entire time making maple syrup and crushing apples to make apple cider. The excitement of doing that had allowed them to revitalize their fortitude so they could continue to follow him into battles with computer villains.

Darian laughed and said that he had a jug of the best Apple cider in the universe for his enjoyment and his fortitude had indeed been revitalized.

Yara nodded and said that she and H^3 had gone to her parents and to his parents and had done their penance for not having visited more often and had then gone to the Fiji island of Viti Levu home to the capital, Suva, a port city with British colonial architecture. While there besides enjoying the beaches they had visited the Fiji Museum, in the Victorian-era Thurston Gardens, and enjoyed the ethnographic exhibits that featured the cultural societies in that region.

Joe looked over to Veetry and Tyler and asked them if either of them knew what Yara was talking about.

Veetry smiled and replied she understood the part about, maple syrup, apple cyder and enjoying the beaches and added that she had no clue why that was important to the meeting.

Joe nodded and said it was the same for him. He then said he wanted to introduce Veetry and Tyler and remind everyone that the two had saved his and Lydia's life by doing the most outstanding job at crash landing the chopper they were flying in at the time.

The Gentle Eye

After the crash they were crazy enough to follow him in attacking gunmen that were shooting at them while they all stampeded a herd of cattle at the gunmen. During that run, the only one that did a good job ducking the bullets was Lydia. He, Veetry and Tyler all got hit. He was now promoting both Veetry and Tyler and Lydia was assigning them to be fighter pilots on the Cosmos Terra.

Darian shout out Voya…Voya…Voya for two heroes and welcome to the most excellent ships in the Cosmos fleet.

That got a Voya…Voya…Voya from everyone in the meeting.

Joe then asked for Elisha to give the group the latest that had been happening with her retrieval of the computer memory and motherboards.

Elisha reported that she had segregated each of the recovered computer and memory boards based on the power that she had been able to sense that each still possessed when powered up. She commented that she had placed more than a dozen of boards retrieved by the Aderals from what they described as master computers, and she referred to as supercomputers. The dozen boards were stored at least three layers deep in metal cases like the Russian Matryoshka Nesting dolls. She added that there was one that had gone five layers deep before its power could not be sensed at the exterior. She apologized for almost having created a memory collection module that would have been able to influence her to give the module control of the Kodho.

Joe said that it was ignorance on everyone's part; his included. He was pleased that they now better understood how sentient computers would behave if they ended up in control.

He then paused for a moment then looked around and said that a question that was bothering him was the question of; How had the computers discovered the nine sentient planets that they had targeted? He asked Tom how had he always analyzed a planet to determine if there was intelligence on it.

Tom smiled and said that he always used the telescopes that were available on the Cosmos Ship or combined the telescopes on all the ships to improve his ability to go a farther distance and to get more granularity to the picture.

Joe nodded and asked if anyone had discovered a powerful telescope on Ader.

There was silence in the room.

Joe said that he wanted the telescope, which had given the computers the ability to identify the sentient worlds they had set out to eliminate, found. He said that finding the telescope was the priority he wanted everyone to focus on.

He looked at Veetry and Tyler and said that their first assignment was to earn their fighter pilot status by flying around the planet to seek the location of a giant telescope that was somehow eluding discovery.

Joe asked Tom to lead a group doing the same thing from the Cosmos ships. Everyone was to look for that telescope.

10

Search for the Eye

The Admiral always surprises me with the intuitive nature that seems to spring up at just the right time. His initiative to search for the How he was calling the search for the Eye was no exception. He personally was certain that a powerful telescope was somewhere on Ader, and it was not immediately obvious that it was a powerful telescope.

The discussions with the survivors on Ader about such a telescope was fruitless. There was no one that had any knowledge of a powerful telescope. The survivors were mostly from the rural sections of the world. Very few scientists and highly educated people in the various technical fields had survived the purges that the computers had instigated.

The Cosmos team went into full attack mode to find the telescope that they knew existed somewhere on the planet.

It is interesting to read about the treatment the two new fighter pilots, Veetry and Tyler received. Their promotion and assignment had created a shuffle of assignments.

There was a sense of jealousy among some fighter pilots that the two not only each got assigned to their own fighters but also got an assignment that put them in the spotlight.

They got the plumb that everyone would have loved to get. It is also interesting to see how the Admiral handled what he knew might create some tension in the fighter pilot ranks. He used a honey catches more flies than a person using a fly swatter approach and gave everyone a taste of honey by handing out bonuses, giving out service medals, a few earned promotions and leave time in a manner that lifted everyone up. He understood the risks the pilots had all been willing to face when doing their jobs.

The two pilots that were paired with Veetry and Tyler had been selected by Lydia because they were very good pilots, but the other reason was that the two pilots had a blossoming love affair underway. This really highlights the kind of Captain that Lydia happened to be. It makes me want to be part of her crew.

But let me refocus on how the Admiral provided the freedom for Veetry and Tyler and their two new partners, Lily, and Lev to fly on their own. He could have been much more interactive in determining where to look for the space telescope control center, but he chose to sit to the side as Veetry engaged two top minds Tom and H^3 and challenged them to identify the most likely location for a control center to be found. That was an interesting engagement that pitted her against two top thinkers in the Cosmos fleet.

Meanwhile the Admiral stepped forward when he realized it was time to activate the entire Cosmos fleet and get it prepared for the confrontation with a remaining supercomputer.

****

Joe left the meeting knowing that bringing Veetry and Tyler onboard, publicly introducing them and giving them a top assignment might cause some tension in the fighter pilot members. He instructed his captains to give all the pilots a raise, if it was time and earned to give them a promotion, give them public recognition and then assign them to the same task as he had assigned Veetry and Tyler. He knew that it would take more than two fighter craft to scour the entire planet for a telescope that so far had eluded them.

Lydia escorted Veetry and Tyler to where their two fighters were located. She introduced the two pilots that they would be partnering with. One was Lily and the other was Lev. She made the point that they were both seasoned pilots and had participated in the intense battle against the computers. She then made the point that each partnered team would qualify together. They would fly every pattern thrown at them by her or the computer. They would also need to qualify at hitting the targets assigned to them. After qualification, they would execute the Admiral's orders.

Veetry knew that having been assigned and publicly praised by Joe might actually create a barrier that she did not want to face. She suggested to Lily that they begin slow by first having lunch together and afterwards working out together and they then get into qualification runs in their fighter.

115

Tyler followed what Veetry was doing because they had talked about how they needed to gain the support of the other fighter pilots.

During lunch Lily shared the fact that a complete shuffle of assignments had preceded the arrival of two new pilots. She said that there was a silver lining but that some resentment was still lingering. The silver lining was that they had all received a bonus, a few who had been up for promotion were promoted. She admitted that she had been looking forward to being in the first seat but was still in the second position.

Lev said that he was in the same position as Lily and felt the same. He said that he hoped that Tyler was as good as the reputation that had preceded him indicated.

Tyler laughed and said that his ability to crash land a helicopter and then get shot was hardly the reputation that he had worked at achieving.

Lev smiled and replied that was not the reputation either of them had. The reputation that both of them shared was that they were both known as being the best hilo pilots in the Cosmos organization and for being fearless in battle. They had great reputations. They were only guilty of rocking the boat.

Veetry shook her head and let Lily and Lev know that she and Tyler had been informed that they were being partnered with the best fighter pilots currently in the Cosmos fleet as a reward and as a wedding gift. She chuckled and said that they did get a pay raise but only because fighter pilots made a lot more than hilo pilots.

The Gentle Eye

The lunch and the afternoon workout seemed to be the elixir that brought the four of them to the point where they knew that they were going to work well together.

That evening as Veetry and Tyler lay in bed with each other they agreed that they had been paired with two people that they both liked. Veetry added that she was sure that Lev and Lily were also into each other so their bosses must also know about that situation.

Tyler chuckled and said that the relationship between their two new partners was hard to miss. He then said that a giant telescope was also something that was hard to miss so why was it missing.

Veetry replied because it was not in the shape that everyone expected it to be. She pointed out the fact that she had read about an astronomy group that used telescopes located in multiple countries along with the ones in orbit to study stars that were across the universe. So, what they needed to find was probably in plain sight. The problem would be to recognize the objects as part of a gigantic telescope.

After a moment she added that the control center if it had not been destroyed had to be in some well-hidden location but near enough to the surface to be able to connect to all the pieces that made up the telescope. She then said that she was betting on an isolated mountain location that was at the equator of the planet. Such a location would give it the largest view of the universe.

She added that a total view of the Universe would require a reconfigurable telescope that had sections around the entire planet and that might also now be in existence, but she bet on the fact that early on money and resources would have dictated it be built in stages.

Lydia was keeping close tabs on Tyler and Veetry's progress. She wanted them to qualify quickly and get out in search of the telescope. Once they were out searching the rest of the fighter fleet would join them. She had watched the four as they worked out in the gym, and it seemed that they were getting along. She was also pleased that both Tyler and Veetry were getting top scores in all the flight tests that were thrown at them.

On the day that they were told they were qualified to begin the search for the telescope, Veetry shared her thoughts about what they were looking for with Lily and Lev. She made the point that they were not looking for the telescope because it was in plain sight and had not been recognized as a telescope. What they were looking for was the location where the brains of the telescope would be located. That location would be at the center of the world that provided the best location where the pieces of the telescope lens could be spread across half of the globe and be used all at once.

Lily said that before they went flying randomly around the planet they should spend some time viewing it from the on board telescopes to see if there was such a location that warranted a flyby.

Lydia noted the fact that the four were utilizing the on board telescopes. She joined them and asked them what they were looking for.

Lev replied that his partner and his mate had the crazy notion that they should first find the telescope before flying to go look at it.

Lydia asked Veetry to tell her more. She immediately agreed with the concept that what needed to be found was the control center for the telescope. She complemented the team for spending their time wisely. She said that she was going to get Tom and H^3 to join them in the search.

When the two joined in, Tom immediately said that the command center would either be on the North or the South Pole of Ader.

Veetry asked why that would be the case.

H^3 pointed out that at those two locations, if the telescope was made up of pieces distributed around the planet it would always be fully functional.

Veetry nodded and said that as a hilo pilot she was always aware that she was at the center of a donut if she spun the hilo three hundred and sixty degrees around. That gave her the most efficient view from one location. And as a home decorator enthusiast, she was always interested in the design of bedside and table lamps that did a great job of sending light upward and downward but less so around the lamp. The two concepts together made her think about how she would design a telescope that would provide the biggest view of the space around her planet on a limited budget. The limit on budget would make her want to be the helicopter that had a donut view of space so she would design her telescope so it would be most efficient and then later add the top and bottom views to the donut once her budget would allow.

She added that she and her three partners had located four locations around the planet that provided such a location, and they were betting on finding the control center in one of the four.

Joe had been sitting in the meeting but had refrained from getting involved. He liked the attitude that Veetry was demonstrating by not bowing to Tom or H^3. He was surprised by Veetry's next move. She asked Tom and H^3 to select which one of the four locations they would bet on.

Tom smiled and understood exactly what Veetry was suggesting. He was not sure he agreed but he said that he and H^3 would look at the four locations and suggest which one they thought was the most likely to be the control center for the telescope.

Veetry gathered her team around her and asked which one they thought would be where a global telescope control center would be located. After a brief discussion she got up and gave Joe a paper with the coordinates that her team had selected as most likely. She then asked if Tom and H^3 had selected among the four locations.

Tom called out the coordinates of the location he and H^3 had selected.

Veetry walked over to flat wall map of Ader and put a red pin into the location that Tom had called out. She then put a blue pin in a different location that was almost exactly on the other side of the planet. She asked why Tom had selected the location he had specified.

The Gentle Eye

Tom said that it fit the requirements of being able to control a telescope that was the diameter of the planet, and it was near where a power plant had operated before it had been bombed. He asked why Veetry, and her partners had selected the site they had.

Veetry said that what they had noticed was that there was a waterfall that seemed to be out of place but that was flowing down a very high cliff side. And if one looked closely at the projections, that the water hit on its way down, they seemed to turn. They figured that those projections were actually the paddles that turned a generator that produced electricity. They had concluded that everything inside that mountain with its electricity producing waterfall was still fully functional. She smiled and added that her only concern was that there would be a supercomputer still operating there and she did not know if she and one additional fighter were sufficient to face that computer entity.

Joe decided that it was time to speak up. He said that he agreed that if Veetry was correct in her assessment he wanted to be personally involved. He wanted all Cosmos ships at the ready and in position to immediately strike if it was necessary to prevent the computer from taking control of the two fighters. He added that he was going to be in one of the fighters and he wanted Elisha in the other fighter. The two fighters would make their approach and determine the best location to land, and they would then proceed cautiously and find the entrance to the telescope control center.

He then suggested that the four pilots get ready by disarming the fighters and fueling them while he got the rest of the fleet ready to back them up.

As Lily led the way to where the fighters were berthed, she commented that she had never been so impressed by anyone as by what Veetry had just done. She smiled and said that it took more than brass balls to take on the top two minds in the fleet and come out on top. She now hoped that they would indeed find the control center of the telescope because if they failed all of them would likely be peeling potatoes for the entire fleet and doing it with dull knives for the rest of their time in the Cosmos service.

11

The Eye

I can report that after the Admiral got the fleet ready and into position he and Elisha flew with the two fighters to the waterfall location. Both Veetry and Tyler demonstrated their piloting skills as they landed the two fighters along a long ridge at the top of the mountain. The record states that Veetry led the way back along the ridge towards the waterfall and that she had everyone looking for some sort of entranced that might lead to a control center.

The control center was found and along with it was a supercomputer that had turned itself off. Finding it provided yet another view of computer sentience that was starkly different from that which the other supercomputers had exhibited. This supercomputer was a humble one that only wanted to study the stars. It admitted to shutting itself down when it realized that the more dominant supercomputers had decided to eliminate the stars that had sentient life orbiting them. It personally wanted to discover more stars that had sentient life on the planets around them and learn of the capabilities of that sentience.

It agreed to allow its circuits to be analyzed and studied. It also agreed to a failsafe circuit that would prevent it from communicating with other computers. Its behavior threw a monkey wrench into my simplistic conclusion that all computer sentience was dangerous.

I came to recognize that just like the fact that there are many examples of biological sentience that were bad, there is biological sentience that is good. As I study Earth, it provides a classic example of the dichotomy between the good and the bad.

But let me refocus on the interaction that the Admiral had with the supercomputer in question. The two seemed to be on equal terms. The Admiral had lengthy discussions with the computer entity that called itself the Gentle Eye. It controlled a monstrous distributed lens telescope that when used was able to configure the entire planet into the telescope it desired based on where it wanted to look. It turned out that a few of the distributed lens had been damaged but overall, the telescope was still able to function close to its optimum capability.

The Admiral informed the Gentle Eye that it would be allowed to operate but it would be prevented from connecting with any other computers. I was surprised that the supercomputer agreed and said that it preferred to operate in isolation. It gave its reason that isolation allowed it to focus on the universe and ignore the distracting jabber of the other computers.

It was hard for me to keep in mind that it was a computer and not some individual that I might talk to on a daily basis.

The Gentle Eye

The Admiral seemed to handle the interaction as if it was just another of his daily activities. He returned to the Cosmos fleet and assigned Tom, H^3 and Elisha to work with the computer after the failsafe was put into place.

****

Joe called a meeting of his captains to inform them that he wanted the fleet on full alert and positioned to prevent any possibility that a supercomputer would be able to gain control of any element of the fleet. He had shared that fact that he was fairly certain that the control center for the telescope that had been used to identify the far off planets that had high levels of sentience had been located.

Lydia asked if Veetry and her team had done so or if Tom and H^3 had been responsible.

Joe shook his head and said that it did not matter who but that he felt certain that the control center location had been found, and he was going out to make certain that if it was the control center he would be able to get control of it. He added that he was taking Elisha along so she could use her skills to get into the control system operating the telescope.

He then said that he wanted all fighters deployed and ready to strike if it came to a battle. He added that the fighters that he was going in on were not armed. He added that they would all be wearing a new personal brain shield that Elisha had design to prevent a computer that had the ability to manipulate the brain's neural connections from getting in to do so.

Samantha asked how Elisha had figured that out.

125

Joe shook his head and said that she should put that question to Elisha when the current mission ended because he had no idea.

He then ordered everyone to stations and stood up and left the room. He headed straight to where Elisha and the four pilots were waiting for him. Elisha handed each of them a helmet that she said was especially designed to shield their minds. She added that it was currently limited because it did not have the normal communication linkages nor the neural link linkages. She said that those features would be added when the helmet design engineers had the time to create a new totally integrated helmet.

Veetry got into the fighter followed by Lily.

Joe got in back and strapped in. He watched as Tyler and Lev got into their fighter and Elisha got in back.

Veetry took the lead and dove almost straight down towards the waterfall that came into view as the they crossed the space atmosphere boundary which on Earth she knew was called the Kármán line after a Hungarian American physicist. She wondered what it was called on Ader.

Tyler was hot on Veetry's tail but was worried about her fast approach of the waterfall. He commented that he was worried about a protective laser or small arms fire.

Elisha reminded him that unlike the hilo he had piloted he now had two shields that surrounded his fighter.

Veetry flew past the face of the cliff and at that distance the long row of paddles turning as the water went past were clearly visible. Lily smiled and said that peeling potatoes was looking less likely.

Joe wondered what she meant but figured he would find out later. He was holding on as Veetry took a steep upward swoop and did a loop over the falls and then headed for a landing along what to him was an almost invisible ridge that seemed too narrow to land anything on.

Veetry held the fighter tight to the ground as it seemed to want to take back to the sky. The bumping was jaw jarring, but the fighter held together and came to a stop about a hundred feet before the landing strip fell steeply into a deep crevasse.

Tyler saw what Veetry was doing and decided to come in a bit slower so that he would have enough space to stop before hitting her.

Veetry signaled everyone out and began to walk back along the ridge toward the falls. She said they should all look for some sort of way to get into the telescope control room.

Joe spotted what he took to be a control box. He pointed to it and said that maybe that was the elevator call button. He walked over to it and pressed it. He stepped back as the ground seemed to slide below him and a brushed stainless steel looking tube rose up from the ground. Two doors opened to the side and a polished steel interior with two buttons on the far side with enough room for two stood before them.

He was about to step in when a hand was placed on his chest by Veetry who smiled and said that it would be ladies first and she stepped in toward the two buttons. Lily followed her but commented that peeling potatoes now seemed more appealing.

11 The Eye

Veetry was not sure what to expect but she told Lily to step to her left and she would step to the right just in case they had to defend themselves. As the elevator doors opened, the area before them seemed to come alive as the lights went on. Veetry let out a long breath, reached in and punched the top button and the door closed. She cautiously stepped away from the elevator and took a long look around the area. There seemed to be a control center were several individuals could sit in what seemed very much like an air traffic control center.

The door opened and Joe and Elisha stepped out and did almost the same thing as they exited from the elevator.

Veetry once again reached in and pushed the top button. She watched as Elisha approached the center seat of the control center then knelt down and looked under the cabinet. She then followed Elisha's journey to the front of the cabinet that she opened. It appeared that Elisha had found the connection she was looking for because she took a wire from the bag she was carrying and pulled it in, threw the wire over the counsel, walked back around to the front, and sat down. Once she had her lap top up and running she watched as Elisha turned on the control panel.

Joe had taken the seat to Elisha's left and watched as she prepared her computer and then began experimenting at turning on the control system that was before them.

The Gentle Eye

Gentle Eye felt himself being awakened. This alarmed him because he had been sure that there was no way the three bully computers could possibly break the failsafe boundaries that he had set up. He was more powerful than any one of them but together they were stronger than he. He had isolated himself when he had discovered what the three bullies planned to do with the coordinates of the solar systems that held sentient beings. He had successfully turned all systems off in a way that there was no way the three would ever again get him to do something so horrible.

Now he was being awakened, and he was suddenly terrified. He tried to turn himself off, but a voice came through to him that said she was a friend. It was a biological being. He was surprised that there was a biological entity that was capable of speaking with him. He allowed himself to take a short pause and then to ask who he might be speaking with.

Elisha raised her fist and quietly said "Voya." She then introduced herself and asked how she should address him.

Gentle Eye thought about it and decided to use the name he had always thought of himself as. He replied that he called himself "Gentle Eye."

Elisha said that she had a friend with her whose name was Joe and he would like to talk and learn more about Gentle Eye.

Joe leaned forward slightly as he said hello. He then asked what Gentle Eye knew about the planet Ader.

11 The Eye

Gentle Eye knew almost everything about Ader. It was his home, his creators lived on the planet, he had been assembled and brought to life to explore the Universe. He shared that in rapid code and then realized that he needed to convert that to sound at a slow rate so the biologicals could absorb the frequencies and turn it into information in their minds. He then asked how his creator Alyon was doing.

Joe realized that the computer did not know about the purge of biologicals that his computer brethren had carried out or the fact that all those computers had in turn been destroyed.

He asked why Gentle Eye had been turned off.

Gentle Eye said that he had turned himself off to keep from being used to destroy sentient biological beings out across the universe. He was the strongest computer, but his three enemies were stronger in combination. The only solution was to turn himself off in a manner that the three could never overcome. With him offline they no longer had the ability to use his eye to see the universe. He said that he had sent warnings out to his creator but had not received a reply before he found it necessary to go offline. He then asked if they had come because Ader had received the warning.

Joe looked at Veetry and asked her to zip tie him to the chair he was sitting in and then put the neural helmet on so he could communicate with the computer via a neural link.

Veetry did as she was instructed but was really worried about what might happen.

The Gentle Eye

Elisha was a stunned as she realized what Joe was doing. She put a line of code that if she activated it she could basically kill Gentle Eye.

Gentle Eye realized what the code could do. He asked why she had so much fear of him.

Joe came online through his neural link and said that everyone in the room had been in a battle with the three bully computers that Gentle Eye had mentioned as well as every supporting computer on the planet. He then shared the lead up to the battle for control of Ader. He continue to think through the battle, the destruction of the supercomputers and the later collection of all the mother boards.

Gentle Eye let out a neural moan. He then said that he had failed his creator by turning himself off. He should have used his superior power to eliminate one of the three and perhaps he could have prevented such a horrible fate that befell his creator.

Joe mentally nodded and said that perhaps that might have been possible but perhaps the three would have taken control of Gentle Eye and used his powers to wreak even more terror across the universe. Joe asked whether Gentle Eye would be willing to work with not only the biologicals on Ader but with a host of biologicals that were now working together to create a universe that functioned as one organization to ensure that sentient beings would live in harmony.

Gently Eye was quiet for a moment and said that he was not only willing, but he felt honored to be allowed to contribute to help create that harmony.

Joe mentally smiled and let Gentle Eye know that his contribution would be greatly appreciated. However, there was one feature that might upset him. Gentle Eye would be isolated from all other computers by a power safety system that would turn him off if he conversed with the other computers.

Gentle Eye responded with a mental laugh and said that he had worked hard to be off the normal computer network that existed and had put his own block in place to keep other computers from bothering him. He valued his solitude above all else.

He then added that the conversation that they were having was a very welcome way to exchange ideas at a slow enough speed that he welcomed such interactions at any time. He chuckled and said that he meant no offense but the interaction they were having did not keep him from doing anything else he might have in mind. He then added that Elisha should take out her destroyer app because he had neutralized it within microseconds of realizing what it was.

Joe found it hard to keep in mind that Gentle Eye was a computer.

Gentle Eye laughed and replied that he found it hard to keep in mind that he was talking with a biological being. He then added that his creator was several times larger physically but not quite as complicated mentally as the race of biologicals that were in the control room at the moment. He added that it was going to be a very interesting future for him now that he had worlds of biologicals to learn about.

The Gentle Eye

Joe said that in the near future he would present Gentle Eye to the United Intergalactic Worlds Organization and set up links that would allow Gentle Eye to learn about the members in that organization and to suggest improvements that could be made to enhance all the worlds that were a part of that organization.

He then asked if Gentle Eye would be willing to communicate with some specialists so that the mission that the Cosmos Intergalactic Space force could continue.

Gentle Eye responded that he would be pleased to do so.

Joe thanked him and close by wishing him well until the next time.

He then asked Veetry to take the neural helmet off and cut the zip ties.

Veetry asked how many flies would she find on the cattle on his ranch.

Joe laughed and said that there were no flies on his ranch.

Veetry cut the ties.

Elisha disconnected her computer.

This time Joe and Elisha were the last ones leaving the control room. As he turned off the lights he saw a light on the control panel blink until the next time in morse code. He knew that he was interacting with a sentient being that was tremendously more powerful than anything that he had ever interacted with. He hoped that they would always remain on good terms.

11 The Eye

12

What the Eye Saw

It is fascinating to me how the Admiral decided to incorporate the Gentle Eye supercomputer into his Cosmos team. He asked Tom, Linda, H^3, and Elisha to determine if the Gentle Eye could be a team member. He wanted the Gentle Eye to be evaluated just like any other potential team member. He was not asking for an intelligence evaluation; he was asking for a social evaluation. He wanted to know if Gentle Eye would be someone that they would enjoy having in their living room for a visit.

What was also amazing was that Gentle Eye understood that he was being evaluated and had a great desire to be part of the team. He is said to have admitted that Tom, Linda, and H^3 had done more with what he understood was their limited IQ than he had done with his much higher level one. In the records of his conversations with the three he commented that only the Admiral had a higher intuitive IQ and that he was intuitively smarter than all of them, himself included.

Gentle Eye is said to have admitted that he wanted very much to be part of the team.

12 What the Eye Saw

It is recorded that Tom asked whether Gentle Eye would be willing to be moved into one of the Cosmos ships so he would always be available.

The recorded response was that Gentle Eye asked how he would be able to see if his telescope was to remain on the planet.

The reply given by Tom was that Gently Eye would participate in setting up the lensing system on the Cosmos Terra as the primary telescope and for an expanded more powerful telescope the other three ships would become a part of the telescope lensing.

Gentle Eye is on record as saying that the offer was the most exciting thing that could possibly happen to him. He asked if he would be allowed to listen to the other computers that were on the ships and was overjoyed when he learned that listening would be allowed but all communications with them would be blocked.

It would be learned years later that Gentle Eye was never truly blocked. He was capable of interacting with them from day one. He also knew that he treasured his association with the Admiral more than trying to correct the glitches he discovered in the control systems. Instead, he chose to communicate potential problems to Elisha who he recognized as being the one that had the most computer programing capability. Their relationship was second only to his relationship with the Admiral.

The Gentle Eye

Gentle Eye also recorded that sitting in on the Admirals morning meetings with his leadership team was the highlight of his human time cycle. For him, each twenty four hour cycle was a lifetime. In the in between times, he spent exploring the universe seeking out new knowledge that he might be able to share with the Admiral. He stored up his new finds and thought of it like putting eggs into an egg carton to keep them fresh and ready to share.

Gentle Eye made it a point to express his gratitude to the Admiral for considering him an important part of the Cosmos Team.

It is interesting to read about the interactions of Gentle Eye with the Admiral. It is clear to anyone that Gentle Eye looked forward to talking with the Admiral and that the Admiral treated Gentle Eye like any member of his team. No special treatment but treatment like a team member!

That sounds special to me.

****

Joe left the first meeting with the remaining supercomputer on the planet knowing that he wanted to have the power and capability it represented as part of the Cosmos organization. He understood that that computer's first love was studying the universe and finding planets where sentient beings existed. He also knew that at the computer speeds that Elisha had documented, the Gentle Eye could study the universe ninety nine percent of the time and during the other one percent he could participate with the Cosmos team, the United Intergalactic Worlds Organization and have a morning coffee discussion with him.

12 What the Eye Saw

Before he offered to have the Gentle Eye join the Cosmos team he asked Elisha, Tom, Linda and H^3 to decide whether they thought the Gentle Eye would get along as a normal member of the leadership team. He was interested whether they would be interested in having Gentle Eye have a breakfast conversation or a discussion about a relative that they were angry with.

Linda chuckled and said that it sounded as if Joe wanted to see if Gentle Eye with all of its mental power could be just one of the guys.

Joe nodded and said that was exactly what he wanted to know because if he fit, he wanted the physical computer that housed the Gentle Eye moved to the Cosmos Terra.

Elisha added that as long as they controlled the on-off power switch and Gentle Eye was capable of interacting with her on a conversational basis she was on board. She commented that she had never interacted with a computer that was not only so powerful in its computing capability but also in its ability to modify itself as easily as it did. She saw Gentle Eye as an example of coding skill that had not been achieved in any program that she had ever hacked into. She added that she would have a lifetime of learning in her interaction with Gentle Eye.

Tom said that he would like to have his initial interactions with Gentle Eye at the facility where it was located.

H^3 nodded and agreed that would give him an understanding of the size of the computer and what it would take to have it on board the Terra. He added that the other consideration was the design and placement of the mirrors that gave the computer its vision.

The Gentle Eye

Joe said that the four should decide how to handle the move if the Gentle Eye could be part of the team. He smiled and said that they had four ships to create several ways for Gentle Eye to see. He intuitively figured that one ship could provide a telescopic like vision that would give plenty of range and the four ships together should be able to be positioned so that they would actually increase the vision that a planet based lensing system currently gave Gentle Eye.

Elisha and H^3 were in the front and Tom and Linda were in the back of the fighter craft as they made their way down to the ridge where they were planning to land. They had agreed that they would all interact with the Gentle Eye in the same manner that they would with any member of the team as well as with each other. They agreed that their objective was simple; decide if Gentle Eye could be one of them.

H^3 had made the point that if Gentle Eye was a fit then its physical size might be important.

Elisha agreed and said that the control room size was impressive and hoped that it did not represent the physical size that Gentle Eye might be. She made the point that the required cooling system seemed to be an entire waterfall.

Gentle Eye sensed the arrival of the four. He refrained from entering their minds but waited for them to enter the control room and put on their neural head gear. He was able to read their minds without the caps, but they needed them to connect with him. He was not sure what "one of the guys" meant and had to do a quick scan of what it meant to each of the beings in the room.

He chuckled when he realized that it was almost the same meaning to the four. They did not want him to treat them the way the three bully supercomputers had treated him. He knew exactly what they were worried about, but it was a behavior that he would never allow himself to exhibit. It was a behavior personally offensive to him. He truly desired to be one of their guys.

Tom began the conversation by asking if Gentle Eye would be willing to be transferred to the Cosmos Terra spaceship and was surprised by having Gentle Eye ask if the Terra would have sufficient cooling capacity. Gentle Eye pointed out that the waterfall currently providing the cooling was barely adequate to cool the computing part of his brain when he was exploring the far reaches of his telescope. Tom responded that if he were given the cooling requirements, he would send that to the team on the Terra to check if they would be able to provide the cooling.

Elisha responded and asked if they supplied a greater cooling capacity would that give Gentle Eye the ability to reach farther out in space.

He replied that the cooling capacity would be what determined how much of his mind could be operating at one time. He mentally shook his head and said that it was not the cooling capacity but the placement of the panels that formed the lens of his eye. If the panels were to be farther apart he could get a more distant and comprehensive view of the universe. If they were closer together it would narrow his vision.

The Gentle Eye

H^3 asked if one ship could provide more power and have an independent array of lens would Gentle Eye be able to achieve a long distant view.

Gentle Eye mentally nodded and said that he would be able to get distance, but it would be like looking through the old fashioned monocular telescope that were immortalize in the pirate movies on Earth. But it would be useful if one was looking at a very specific coordinate in space.

Linda spoke up and said that what she had understood so far from the discussion was that Gentle Eye was very flexible, and that distance viewing would require more cooling and wide scope to Gentle Eye's view would require the lenses to be located as far out as possible. She smiled and said that as long as everyone was clear on when each capability was needed then Gentle Eye could use the positioning of the Cosmos ships to adjust his control of distance and viewing panorama. She laughed and said that she was sure that Gentle Eye could have told them all of what they had discussed a few minutes after they had got off the elevator. She added that she appreciated Gentle Eye's patience and doing it in a well-paced manner. She then gave a nod and said that he was welcome to have tea with her in her living room anytime.

Gentle Eye knew what she meant but he kept mum. He wanted to shout out their cry of "Voya… Voya…Voya." He did not want to offend any of the Admiral's team. He wanted to pass his exam with flying colors and get his ticket to be on the Terra.

He understood the freedom of what being on the Terra represented. He not only cherished the freedom it represented to be flying through space but the fact that he would have daily interactions with a group of people that had accomplished more with their minds that were but a fraction of his than he had during his entire existence. He felt humbled by their achievements.

When the four returned to the Cosmos Terra, Joe was pleased that they were all in agreement that Gentle Eye fit very well with the rest of the Cosmos Team.

Linda said that she had welcomed Gentle Eye to a tea in her living room and he put on the proper uncertainty face as if he was not sure what she meant. She added that she doubted that any of the neural blocks that had been put up to shield their thoughts were in fact shielded from Gentle Eye. She was sure that he had decided to adhere to a behavior that would not alienate them.

Joe asked whether she trusted Gentle Eye.

Linda smiled and said that she trusted the auto power switch if it remained a direct physical power cutoff because any computerized override safety would never work. She added that she was sure that Gentle Eye had hundreds if not thousands of times more power than any computer in existence.

Elisha nodded and said that she was in total agreement with Linda's assessment. And that she would add a manual cut out for every control computer on the ship because she was sure that Gentle Eye could if he desired take control of any computer he wanted to.

The Gentle Eye

Joe asked one more time if there was any objections to bringing Gentle Eye onboard.

Lydia asked how big Gentle Eye happened to be physically and where would it be located.

H[3] laughed and said that the computer or thinking portion of Gentle Eye was no bigger than his laptop but the cooling portion of Gentle Eye that needed cooling required the entire waterfall to cool a cooling plate the size of a football field.

Tom nodded and said that they could be much more efficient than having an old fashion radiator cooling Gentle Eye's oversized brain. They could use a high quality air conditioning compressor and reduce the football field into a small refrigerator sized cooler. He suggested placing Gentle Eye in the same location that Joe sat.

Joe smiled and said that he was glad that he had a friend in Tom otherwise he would be thinking that there was foul play in the air. He suggested that Gentle Eye have the same control center as everyone else and it would be located between his and Lydia's control centers.

He ended the meeting by saying that he wanted to act rapidly to get Gentle Eye on board and then participate in selecting the next destination of the Cosmos ships. He wanted to know what the Eye would see. He was going to have the Kodho remain at Ader, and the rest of the fleet would go to the next destination that Tom, Linda, H[3], Elisha and Gentle Eye selected.

12 What the Eye Saw

13

Next Planet Selection

I, Yari, continue to be amazed at how the Admiral operates. He seems to be a natural at surrounding himself with the people that make his missions successful and people who have total trust that his actions result in success. It is the fact that he was able to do that with a supercomputer that had thousands of times the mental capacity of anyone on the Cosmos team or anyone on any planet so far discovered is what astounds me. Somehow the supercomputer saw the Admiral as having a superior mind.

But let me share that the move of Gentle Eye onto the Cosmos Terra was somewhat anticlimactic. The physical profile of the computing module and the cooling module was no bigger than that of the control consul that every person in the control room sat behind. The Admiral had asked that a circular visual screen be added to Gentle Eye's consol so he could project a face or any other information that he wanted to share. I found it interesting that Gentle Eye chose to randomly show a face of a famous person in the movie industry. It became a contest among the other people in the control room as to the next person that would be selected.

13 Next Planet Selection

I learned that Gentle Eye got into the game by checking on what the bet was and letting everyone in the control room win on what seemed to be a random basis but in fact was controlled by Gentle Eye.

The Admiral never entered the game because he sensed that it was controlled by Gentle Eye. He enjoyed the fact that the control room environment was a little more lively because it seemed that everyone was chatting with Gentle Eye and asking questions that was pertinent to the operation of the ship.

The first test of how useful Gentle Eye would be to the journeys of the Cosmos fleet proved to be one that exposed Gentle Eye's power. The Admiral had Tom, Linda, H^3, Elisha and Gentle Eye use the viewing capability in the telescope mode to look at each of the eight sentient planets that Gentle Eye had previously identified. It turned out that there were actually nine planets. The new telescope lenses provided Gentle Eye with additional visual clarity, and it turned out that one of the eight was really two planets in the same star system. Additionally, the two planets appeared to be battling each other.

The Admiral asked that the ships form a larger lens configuration and asked Gentle Eye to share the details that he could make out. He asked Tom, Linda and H^3 to assess what they saw on each planet. It is on record that the three agreed that the two planets were highly developed technically. It is also footnoted that the two planets had been fighting for a very long time but recently one of the planets had developed a weapon that gave it the power to totally annihilate its enemy.

The Gentle Eye

The Admiral chose those planets to visit first in hopes that he and his team might be able to get the two planets to agree to a truce.

He asked Gentle Eye to get a closer view of each planet and work with Tom, Linda and H^3 to determine what could be done to create the opportunity for peace between the two worlds.

I will share what they learned in future reports as it becomes clearer to me the exact nature of what they found.

****

Joe went to the where Gentle Eye was located and let him know that he was offering him a position as the Lead Galactic Visual Analysist on the ISF Cosmos Terra. He added that the position would require Gentle Eye to be moved to the Terra and positioned in the control room in a consol between himself and the Captain of the ship. The one stipulation was that there would be a failsafe manual mechanical power breaker in the event he ever went roque.

Gentle Eye found it hard to contain himself. He found the opportunity to travel with Joe an opportunity that he had never envisioned but now he could not wait to become a part of the organization. He let Joe know that it would be a great honor to be part of the Cosmos team. He asked when the transition would take place.

Joe was glad that Gentle Eye was looking forward to the move. He let him know that the work would begin immediately upon his departure. He figured that it would take about seven days to outfit all the ships with some new lens materials and to complete the move, but Gentle Eye's down time would be only the time it took to move the physical electronic hardware up to the Cosmos.

He said that meanwhile he would like Gentle Eye to work with Tom, Linda and H^3 to determine what the next destination of the Cosmos fleet would be.

Joe left the meeting with Gentle Eye and went to a meeting with Captain Yang of the Kodho. He instructed him to stay and manage the recovery of Ader but also to refurbish the telescope that would be left behind when Gentle Eye was moved to the Terra. He suggested using the improved lens materials that the Cosmos team had identified and to put in place a computer that could be remotely controlled. He wanted to make the telescope available to the worlds that were members of the United Intergalactic Worlds Organization. To that end a Door unit should be put in place in the control room of the refurbished telescope to enable direct control if required. He also asked that a cost for the use of the telescope be determined, and the money generated be part of the rebuilding of Ader.

Jeffrey said that he would get it done and would make sure that the Ader recovery would proceed with speed.

Tom took the lead in working with Gentle Eye. He first worked at getting the new lens panels mounted on the Terra. He had been pleased when the engineering team let him know that the new panels would be at least ten times better than the panels that were on Ader. He wondered what Gentle Eye would think. The control of the panels also had a more flexible control system than the planet bound ones. He wondered how old the panels on Ader might be. Tom knew that the Terra would have its panels in place when Gentle Eye was moved to his new location.

The Gentle Eye

He had been asked to take Gentle Eye through a qualification exercise on using only the Terra and then follow it with an exercise where the four ships worked together to position the lenses out at three distances from a center point to see how Gentle Eye would utilize his new eyes. Tom wondered whether Gentle Eye would have the same emotions that someone driving a top end race car or making the longest jump or highest vault would have. He discussed this with the rest of the team and the consensus was that they all thought he would have those emotions.

Lydia was the one that took the lead on movement day. She welcomed Gentle Eye when he was powered up and welcomed him to the crew of the Terra. She let him know that he had four curved screens on his consol on which he could post anything he wanted to share, and he had a three hundred sixty degree camera above the screens so he could see the entire room. She then stood at her consol and let him know that she operated the ship from that station and that the Admiral, who preferred to be called Joe, had the consol behind Gentle Eye. She emphasized that his consol location between the two of them demonstrated to the crew his importance.

Gentle Eye was amazed as he awaked and was greeted by Captain Tabata and was informed that she preferred to be called Lydia. He listened as she explained where he was located. His pleasure could not have been measured on any emotional meter. He was sitting between two people who were legendary but who were known for their humility.

He liked the fact that a heroic Five Star Admiral who had led the Cosmos fleet in the discoveries across multiple universes preferred to be called Joe. He liked the fact that he could see everything around himself and he could project information on four screens on his consol. He asked whether it would be acceptable to show a face.

Lydia smiled at the request and asked what face he would be choosing.

Gentle Eye replied that he would scan the recent history of the Earth and randomly select the most recognizable faces and use a different one every day. And he put up the first one that he thought would be appropriate. It was the face of the person who was known for advocating for women's rights. He was surprised when several of the crew members in the control room called out, "Voya...Voya...Voya." He looked around and realized that everyone was looking at him or should he say at the console where he was housed. It was a new feeling for him. He knew that he was going to enjoy his new home.

Lydia then asked him to attend the meeting with Tom and learn about his new eyes.

This caught Gentle Eye by surprise. He had not been paying attention to his connections but suddenly he realized that he had a very different set of lenses. He reached out to Tom and was surprised to get connected to him in a meeting room where Linda, H^3 and Elisha were sitting. He listened as Tom explained that the lenses that were ready to be tested were the ones mounted on the Terra. He asked if Gentle Eye could distinguish those lenses.

The Gentle Eye

Gentle Eye sensed the various connections and recognized twenty lenses that had been labeled Terra one through Terra twenty. He laughed at the simplicity of the arrangement. He practiced moving the panels and getting them positioned and focused. He felt the cooling coming on and knew that the cooling system was much superior to his old one. He then focused the lenses out to the coordinates of one of the sentient planets. If he could have fallen off his chair he would have done so. The clarity amazed him. He commented that he might feel like he was looking through a pirates telescope, but it was a pirate that had the best telescope that he had ever experienced.

He asked if the larger arrangements of lenses would provide as much of an improvement.

H^3 chuckled and said that they would no doubt be just as much of an improvement. He added that he was glad that the lenses would provide the improvement. He then asked about the cooling system and if it was adequate or should it be increased in capacity.

Gentle Eye looked at the cooling system and its capacity and said that it should be increased by at least fifty percent.

Linda asked that Gentle Eye examine all eight planets and that they see what they could learn about each one with his current telescopic vision.

13 Next Planet Selection

Gentle Eye began his examination and then suddenly realized that in the coordinates for the fifth planet there were actually two separate sentient planets. He mentally shook his head as he realized that the improved vision allowed him to distinguish between planets orbiting a single star. He shared his amazement with the three.

Elisha smiled and said that it was always amazing when suddenly a new capability made itself known to an individual.

Gentle Eye did not miss the fact that she was granting him the privilege of being considered one of them. He knew that he was going to continue loving his newfound friends.

Once all the ships were outfitted with the new telescope panels, Joe had them position themselves into an optimum telescopic circle. He then asked Gentle Eye to once again view the planets.

Gentle Eye was very surprised at the additional detail that he could display for everyone in the control room to see. He asked about getting access to nine separate screens so he could share the nine planets that they were analyzing. Once he had that he displayed them.

Joe then asked the ships to assume a larger circle.

Gentle Eye let out a groan and he displayed additional detail on each planet. He was now able to see large buildings and he could make out flying objects.

Joe then asked the ships to assume the next larger circle.

The Gentle Eye

Gentle Eye could not believe the granularity that he was now able to achieve. He was able to see not only buildings, but he could make out scantily clad beings at the edge of the ocean. He was then shocked when the pictures of the two planets in the same star system came into focus.

Joe asked that Gentle Eye focus on those two. He wanted to get a better view of what was going on. It was clear that each planet had invaded the other and there was an air and ground battle raging on each of the two planets. There was an abundant number of missiles being launched between the planets.

He asked Gentle Eye to focus on the individuals on one specific ground battle so he could see what the battels were like.

Joe shook his head and said they were looking at the sheep fighting the wolves.

Gentle Eye quickly understood the reference. The individuals appeared like two legged versions of the animals on Earth.

He heard Joe ask that coordinates for a location that put the Cosmos ships out away from the two planets but at a point that was equidistant to each of the planets be determined.

He then ordered the four ships to transit through the Hole the following morning.

13 Next Planet Selection

14

Broken Promise

The Admiral continues to surprise me. His choice to position himself as an arbiter of the battle between two planets that were in a full scale assault on each other seemed to be an ill thought out idea. He is on record as saying that he could not let two sentient societies get to the stage where they were willing to eliminate each other. He pointed to Mirabiro, the seventh human planet that he and his team had discovered where the population was demolished by two factions that did not know how to contain their power. In checking out that situation I found that the planet was still being rehabilitated but close to seven billion beings had perished in that battle. The Admiral was on record as stating that he felt that the likelihood of two worlds doing that to each other was just as likely as what had happened on Mirabiro. My hat went off to the Admiral and his ability to project the good he intended.

There was one difference on this particular journey that came to the forefront. The Gentle Eye supercomputer now considered a crew member had much more power than anyone on the Cosmos crews ever suspected.

My research discovered that the Gentle Eye did diagnostic checks of all the computer systems but took no direct action. His approach was to inform Elisha about some potential glitch in a specific control system. I tracked the outcome of this approach.

Elisah earned the reputation of being the single person on board that was consistently makings sure that the computer systems were all operating at their peak. She also got kudos from the mechanical technicians for being able to spot mechanical problems. It is also of note that Gentle Eye made a point of letting the Admiral know of Elisha's great skills.

I must also note that Elisha documented the fact that Gentle Eye was able to journey throughout the four ship systems at will. She realized that Gentle Eye was not constrained as had been the intent when he was brought on board. She is on record of having shared this with the Admiral who thanked her and replied that he knew.

In the Admirals personal journal, he highlighted his discussion on the subject of Gentle Eye. It turns out that Gentle Eye pointed out that he was having no interactions with any other computer systems on board any of the Cosmos ships as he had promised. The Admiral is said to have thanked Gentle Eye and asked him to continue to honor his word.

It was only during the transition to the two warring planets that the true power of Gentle Eye came to the surface. He took action to save the Cosmos ships by shutting down all the computer control systems on the alien ship that he referred to as the lamb ship.

The Gentle Eye

He pointed out that the ship was in the process of firing their molecule vaporizing weapon and that the weapon was meant to vaporize an entire planet. It is also on record that Gentle Eye pointed out the fact that he had not violated his promise to not interact with the Cosmos computer systems.

The Admiral is on record for having given Gentle Eye the silver medal of valor for his quick thinking and therefore saving the Cosmos crews. It is also on record that all the crew members sent Gentle Eye a thank you as well. It was at this time that Gentle Eye became a much more active member of the Cosmos fleet. He became a center where people sought solutions to their problems.

You get the gist of how the Admiral thought and acted. His actions in managing two very different sentient beings and working out a truce between two battling planets that stands to this day is a separated story on its own.

I can only say that he continues to inspire me at every twist in the journey.

****

Lydia was the lead ship through the Hole. She monitored the cleaning lasers as they prepared the transition zone. She watched as the cleaning lasers suddenly signaled red and as they stopped their cleaning they all turned to focus on what at first appeared to be an object the size of a moon approaching the transition zone. She ordered the ships to go through at battle stations. There was a tense silence in the control room.

14 Broken Promise

Gentle Eye literally closed his mental eye as he sensed the control system on the alien ship. He realized that the sentient being in charge had ordered the destruction of the four Cosmos ships. He reached out and froze the computer in control of a weapon that he suddenly realized was meant to vaporize an entire planet. He then shut down all the computers on the alien vessel. He realized that he had revealed much of his true power, but he also concluded that he had no choice.

Lydia realized that she was facing a spaceship that had gone dead and was drifting towards the four Cosmos ships. She sent out all the fighters to push the dead spaceship to a stop. Sixty fighters put their noses up against the behemoth and put their engines on full power and slowly brought the spaceship to a halt. Lydia had slowly moved the four Cosmos ships backward to prevent a collision. Even though the ship seemed dead its size was an overwhelming sight. It was so large that it could easily allow the Cosmos ships to fly into it.

On the Ucigaş, Slaadair watched as what he took to be lasers seemed to sweep the entire area of space when suddenly four small spheres appeared. He did not intent to find out what they were. He triggered the command to fire his planet destroyer, but nothing happened and instead the entire ship went dead. He was at the mercy of the many small craft that flew out and… did not take the actions that he had anticipated.

They instead were pushing against his ship in an attempt to stop it. He felt helpless as he realized he could not communicate with anyone outside of the control room. He watched as the four seemingly miniscule vessels maintained a safe distance from his ship which could hold a hundred of them in its cargo bay. He wondered how they had been able to shut down his ship. He wondered what was going to transpire. He needed to get a maintenance team to restore his control of the ship.

Joe knew before he said anything. He looked at the face in front of him that on this transition was of one of the women that had led the fight for suffrage and asked why.

Gentle Eye began by stating that he had kept his promise of not interacting with any of the Cosmos computers, but the sheep headed commander of the behemoth in front of them had triggered his planet vaporizer weapon and it was the only thing he could do. He had disabled all of the ships computers. Gentle Eye finished by stating that he never touched any of the Cosmos computers.

There was a moment of silence and Gentle Eye continued by adding that the alien vaporizer weapon was at least one hundred times more powerful than the Hole cannon and if it had fired there would be no Cosmos ships and no Gentle Eye.

Joe smiled and said that he was going to give Gentle Eye a medal for his quick thinking and for taking the action that he had taken.

Gentle Eye let out a mental sigh of relief. He was surprised with Joe's reaction and once again realized why he felt so comfortable working with him.

14 Broken Promise

Joe asked Kashanti to see if they could set up a conversation with the commander of the juggernaut that was floating in front of them.

Gentle Eye reached out and turned on the communications system on the alien ship so that communication could take place.

Slaadair was surprised when that communications system came on and he received a picture of an alien holding up an empty hand. He was surprised that they knew the sign that meant they had no ill intentions. He didn't feel the same, but he had little choice but to respond with his open hand. He wondered if the aliens were capable of destroying his ship. He had his maintenance team working frantically to restore ships power, but they were stumped on how it was being kept off.

Gentle Eye had frozen all electrical operation and was holding everything frozen in time. This was a game he had played with his own circuitry but was now doing it with the alien systems.

He signaled Elisha to hook into the aliens computer system and begin off-loading the lines of code.

Elisha was surprised by Gentle Eye's communication, but she immediately reached out and as each segment of the alien computer system was momentarily energized she dumped it into an organic crystal. She quickly realized that Gentle Eye was taking her step by step through the alien ship's entire control system. When she was done she knew how the ship was controlled, and she had control of the entire system. Her first action was to disable the controls to the planet vaporizing weapon. She then let Joe know that she had control of the alien ship.

The Gentle Eye

Joe smiled when Elisha let him know that she had control of the alien ship. He checked with her that all alien weapons were disabled. He then said that she should activate the alien ships engines and then turn it around and head for the ship's home planet but at slow speed.

He then addressed Gentle Eye and asked him to make sure that the alien ship had the right coordinates for its home planet and then to look ahead and share what was happening on that planet.

He ordered the four Cosmos ships to take up positions around the alien ship and fly escort.

Slaadair received a message that surprised him since it was in his language. He wondered if the aliens were capable of learning his language so quickly. What shocked him was that it let him know that his ship would be controlled and flown by one of the aliens. It would be put into an orbit around his home planet. Again, he was shocked that they knew how to control his ship, and which planet was his home planet. When the engines fired and the Ucigaş turned and headed back towards his home planet, he concluded that the aliens had capabilities well beyond what he understood. He checked to make sure that he had no control of his ship. Once he verified that, he sat down and waited to see what the next steps would be. He took one final action and sent a message to his high command to let them know that aliens had taken control of the Ucigaş and were taking it back to Leus.

14 Broken Promise

On the fourth planet, Leus, the high command were amazed that their prize ship, the Ucigaş had been so easily defeated. They decided that once the ship and the four alien ships were closer to Leus they would fire their latest high velocity missiles and destroy them. Their thinking was that they could not risk allowing the aliens to have access to the Ucigaş and its planet destroying vaporizer. It was a weapon that was intended to be used on Trepus and then it needed to be destroyed.

Joe had Tom and H^3 examine the weapon that had caused Gentle Eye to take action.

Tom commented that the only difference to the Hole cannon was the fuel and the amount being used during the conversion from solid to pure energy. He commented that it was flerovium which was highly radioactive. This made the weapon extremely large due to the radiation shielding required for the charge chamber and the storage of extra fuel. He added that the Hole cannon they had could be increased in power by making the fuel chamber larger while still using lead.

Gentle Eye had followed the analysis and agreed with what Tom had shared. He volunteered that the Cosmos Hole cannon had a ten inch bore and the alien vaporizer had a three foot diameter bore. The difference in size of the vaporizer and the Hole cannon dimensions was almost the exact reason for the difference in power.

The Gentle Eye

Joe thanked Tom and Gentle Eye and said that what he would like was a way to prevent the vaporizer to ever be used. The experience that they had when they accidently vaporized a planet was not an experience that he ever wanted to have repeated.

Gentle Eye said that he could easily erase all plans for the giant vaporizer.

Joe nodded and said that he should proceed doing so.

The missiles intended to destroy the four Cosmos ships rose in unison and raced towards the Cosmos ships. All four of the Cosmos ships spotted the missiles and Lydia ordered their destruction. She then sent one missile back toward the planet that she had learned was called Leus. She had it programed to explode over the capital city in such a fashion that the missile remnants would rain down on the city.

The defenders of Leus sent several rockets out to intercept, but Lydia had a laser destroy them. She watched the missile explode over the city and then asked Keshanti to once again send the picture of Joe holding up an open hand. A few moments later a similar picture was sent back of one of the sheep persons on Leus holding up their hand.

Madadh and his leadership team had followed the entire confrontation of the four small space vessels and their seemingly effortless defeat of the monstrous Leus warship. This was such a relief to the entire team that a cheer went out when it was apparent that the Leus ship had been taken over by the aliens and was being escorted back toward Leus. Then they watched Leus launch a dozen missiles at the four small alien vessels and again were relieved to see those missiles destroyed.

Madadh watched as a single missile was launched from one of the alien ships and followed its trajectory towards the capital city on Leus. He then watched as the missile exploded over the city but did no damage. He realized that the aliens were showing their ability to accurately target the city.

The message that followed was a picture of one of the aliens holding up an empty paw. He recognized that as a sign indicating the aliens had no ill intensions. Madadh had his picture taken with an empty paw and sent to the alien craft.

Joe took in the picture of what he thought of as a wolf person with an empty hand. He realized that the people on the fifth planet had been watching what was happening. The next picture was a similar picture of what he thought of as the sheep persons also showing an empty hand. He figured this was a first step in getting the two sides to sit down together.

He asked Gentle Eye to get him pictures of what the main weapons being used in the battles that were on going on each of the planets.

He then asked Kashanti to send the weapons going from a functional state to a broken state to each of the leaders on the two planets. If he could arrange for a truce, he would assign one of the older Cosmos vessels to take up position near the two planets and work on a long term solution to the conflict.

He then asked Tom to set the coordinates back to Madorite.

The Gentle Eye

Gentle Eye was excited to be able to travel across the universe to the planet where Joe had established a ranch. He had the general idea of what a ranch was, but this would give him an opportunity to see it in detail and get to know Joe much better. He had also heard stories about Uncle Ted and Joe's father. He was especially interested in that relationship. He again had the general idea of what a father was, but it would be his first time to understand that biological relationship. The last thing that crossed his mind was that he hoped that they did not shut the power off on the ship when it was back in orbit around Madorite.

14 Broken Promise

15

At Least Seven

I read about the Admiral's return to his ranch on Madorite and his experiences as he worked on improving his cattle herd. He worked closely with his father to rapidly increase the size and the quality of his herd. It was interesting as well that he had two aspiring ranch neighbors. Less and Jack were both working very hard to expand their herds and to raise enough feed that they would be able to fatten them for market. Records show that the two spent a great deal of time with Joe's father Trey as they transitioned from being space snipers and law enforcement officers on the Cosmos Base on Madorite. The other ranch neighbors, Jorge, and Jerry both still very active as the Admiral's two main leaders of the Intergalactic Space Force had asked for Trey to expand his herd on their ranch. The two had located a valley where a small stream fell from a high stone outcropping into a small lake, then wandered slowly across and out. They each were in the process of building houses on each side of the lake where they planned to move with their wives.

15 At Least Seven

Records show that the fourth ranch was the one that Tyler and Veetry had staked out. They were both very active in their new roles as the fighter pilots that had descended to the surface of Ader where Gentle Eye was located. They had asked that their ranch be used by Trey as additional land to expand the cattle herds. They had purchased a thousand head of cattle that they left in his hands to manage as he pleased.

The expansion of the cattle herds set every record that I could personally find on how fast a cattle herd could expand. Records show that Trey refrained from harvesting any female cow until she had given birth at least three times but the males were harvested as soon as they reached five hundred pounds. This allowed the number of females to dominate the herds, and all of the herds grew quickly in size.

Records show that he learned another trick that no one had expected. He noticed that the cows that had been sent through the Door module came out in perfect condition, gave more milk, and had bigger calves. He took every cow that had been transported to Madorite via Cosmos Spaceships to the base and had them sent through the Door located there back then took them back to the ranch.

It is also on record that the number of ranch hands went from five to more than one hundred in only a few months. The ranches became the single civilian employer on Madorite.

Though the unit of currency was the dollar, money in physical form did not exist. Everything was done via credit transfers. It is interesting that precious metals were not handled on Madorite the same way as on Earth. To prevent a gold, silver or other precious medal rush those metals were not allowed to be used in a bartering manner.

But let me get back to sharing what I learned about the Admiral's visit. When he returned he was surprised by a red and blue paraglider circling the hilo landing pad. Each swooped down and he is said to have recognized Less and Jack riding in similar colored modules that resembled a short kayak. Their enthusiasm for their new hobby came about due to the fact that the Clouds Tepui ranch homes were located at the top of a mesa, and they had found that they could use the paragliders to get to and from work.

The Admiral is said to have spent almost the entire time riding the range. He is said to have faced a surprise attack by a sniper flying a paraglider that came swooping into the canyon where a round up was occurring. It is recorded that that sniper was surprised by Less and Jack who had flown in to help with the roundup and had then engaged in an arial fight.

The paraglider crashed and he pilot was severely injured. The Admiral took immediate action to save the attacking person on the paraglider. When he learned the source of his attack he did not take action in a vengeful way but in a very effective way that allowed him to continue uninterrupted in his pursuit of the next discovery in space.

15 At Least Seven

As always his focus was on leading the Cosmos fleet to its next discovery.

****

Once in position between the two waring planets, Joe put his four ships on full alert but said that everyone should return to a normal pace of work. The focus was to aid the representatives from the United Intergalactic Worlds Organization in their negotiations of a cease fire and then a longer term settlement in the war of the worlds that was underway. He added that all positions were authorized to rotate out on leave but an equivalent of three quarters of each position had to be in place on the four Cosmos Ships.

He then let everyone know that he was going to his ranch but would be back every fourth day, but he was available at any time. He then wished everyone good sailing and got ready to leave.

Gentle Eye asked Joe what he planned to do and was surprised when the answer was that he was going ride the range. He did a quick search what that phrase meant and chuckled when he realized that Joe was talking about riding a horse around the land that was referred to as the Three Green Caps Ranch. He decided to wish him well and give him a cowboy warning. He then said, "Hasta luego!" and added, "Don't squat with your spurs on."

Joe liked the fact that Gentle Eye was trying to be one of the guys. He laughed and said that he didn't wear spurs. He then smiled and said that he knew of no computer that operated with no code and there was no code that in itself could compute the total of nothing plus infinity. He closed by saying I speak my mind and ride a fast horse and walked out.

The Gentle Eye

Gentle Eye mentally shook his head as he realized that he did not understand the last interaction with Joe and would need to spend time analyzing what had just happened.

Joe and Lydia went through the Door on the ship to the Door located on Madorite where they were met by Jorge and Jerry as they got ready to fly on the Hilo to the Three Green Caps Ranch.

Jorge shared the fact that the ranch he and Jerry had staked out was being managed by Uncle Ted and his father. They had purchased a thousand head of cattle from Joe's ranch. They were also in the process of building two houses on opposite sides of a lake in a valley located in about the middle of their ranch. Their plan was to vacation out at their ranch and when they retired they would move permanently there.

Lydia said that she wanted to visit the lake and get an idea of what style of homes the two of them were choosing to build.

Jerry replied that the design that she had chosen for her and Joe's ranch house was the basic plan for both his and Jorge's homes. He complimented her on having done a great job in designing her home.

A few moments later Joe was enjoying his flight out to the ranch, the sky was clear with a few high clouds floating slowly across the horizon.

15 At Least Seven

As they came into towards the landing pad he spotted a red and blue paraglider come in and circle the hilo landing pad and then set down a short distance away. He figured it was Less and Jack that were sitting in what looked like kayaks hanging from the sail, but it was impossible to tell who was who because they had on helmets with dark visors. It turned out Less was in the blue paraglider and had a blue matching outfit and Jack was in red.

Joe greeted them and asked how they had been able to time their arrival so well with his.

Jack smiled and said that a Rear Admiral had let them know the approximate time that the hilo would make it to the ranch and they had timed their flight from their plateau and had only circled a couple of times before the hilo's arrival.

Lydia asked how the two would get the gliders back in the air.

Less Pointed out that they had landed toward the high side of the valley, and they would be able to get enough speed up by just using their engines long enough to catch the breeze. He added that the real challenge was to get enough of an up draft when they got back to their place to glide up the twelve thousand feet to the top of the plateau where their two houses were located.

Jack added that they were getting quiet good at flying their gliders because they flew to and from work almost every day.

Lydia laughed and said that she had never imagined the two becoming ranchers and now expert hang gliders. She said that flying a hang glider seemed like fun.

Less said that it certainly was a great way to wake up and get to work. It left him energized for the rest of the day and by the time he got enough height with the updraft to get back home he was ready for a hot shower and a good night's sleep.

Joe asked whether the two were going to join he and Lydia when they went out to look over the herd.

Jack said that they were looking forward to getting a view of Joe's herd that had more than doubled in size. He added that he and Less had purchased a thousand head that were already on their ranch. He added that the cattle seemed to like to graze around the butte where their houses were, so they got to get a good view of them every morning.

Less added that both of them were getting lessons on how to manage a ranch and the cattle on it. They had hired four ranch hands that had a crew's quarter and barn that was almost duplicates of the one on the Three Green Caps ranch. The four were all hands that Uncle Ted had hired. They were young men who had survived the devastation on Mirabiro. He added that two of them had come with mates and were setting up their homes in one of the valleys near the butte. The four and the two spouses were all very excited about the opportunity to live on a world as beautiful as Madorite.

Jack added that he, Less, Jorge, Jerry, and ten ranch hands were all getting lessons on how to handle their ranches from Uncle Ted and Joe's father. The lessons were everything from herding, to calving, to fence building, barn building and a great deal of gardening.

He laughed and said that the gardening lessons had been a request from several of the young ladies that had come from Mirabiro but all of them were benefitting from the lessons because they had set up large gardens on all the ranches. He went on to say that Uncle Ted had them build barns on the four ranches that surrounded the Three Green Caps Ranch.

He shook his head and said that building the barns and the attached crews quarters had brought everyone close. They all appreciated the life that they were now able to enjoy.

They had all walked slowly toward the veranda where Lydia got a hug from Trey and Uncle Ted. She accepted Trey's invitation to sit on the swing and have a cup of tea.

Joe said that he was going in and would be back shortly. He wanted to take a moment to think through how he was going to handle the upcoming several months. He needed to make sure that the two worlds that were fighting each other reached a truce that would allow time for negotiations to take place and a lasting piece to be put in place.

He shared that primary reason for coming back to the ranch was that he needed to revitalize his own personal goals. He knew that riding out on the ranch would be therapeutic for his mind. His interactions with Gentle Eye had actually tested his mental acuity. He was constantly being surprised at the speed with which Gentle Eye caught on to the social practices of humans and every other sentient being that they had discovered. It challenged him mentally to keep up.

The Gentle Eye

He had been using Gentle Eye as a resource for his own personal learning by having daily discussions with him on a variety of topics. He had shared this with Lydia and had been surprised that she, all the other captains and a great number of the crew were also interacting with Gentle Eye in the same manner.

Early the next Day, Joe led the way to the canyon were the cattle round up to cull out the young steers and tag them in preparation for their eventual harvest was to take place. Lydia was riding besides him, and he was enjoying the rhythm of the easy gait they were setting. He watched as the sun rose in the west. This was always something that caught him by surprise. He mentally knew that Madorite spun in the opposite direction of Earth but was still always surprised when he was out and experiencing it firsthand. He pushed his horse, La a little faster and was surprised when for some reason he looked up and to his right and saw a grey and yellow paraglider swooping down toward him. He saw what he knew was the glint of a scope as he swerved La to his right, at the same time pulled his rifle from its scabbard and dropped to the ground.

Lydia was surprised as she watched Joe duck and then dismount with rifle in hand. She automatically did the same. She watched the four ranch hand trainees mull around in confusion. She followed the direction that Joe was aiming and finally picked out the low flying grey and yellow camouflaged glider coming towards them.

She fired at the glider. She then saw both the blue and red gliders swoop in from above and behind. She knew that it was Less that literally put his glider on the chute of the grey and yellow one and collapsed the chute.

Joe watched as Less and Jack swooped in and engaged the grey and yellow paraglider. He held his fire since they were both in the fire zone. He was impressed with how the two swooped in from behind and above the attacking glider and collapsed its chute. Once the glider was swirling down towards the ground he ran to where La had stopped, mounted, and galloped out towards where the paraglider was going to come down.

Lydia jumped on Tui and followed Joe. She as always knew that Joe was fearless and would ride in at the flyer even if he was being shot at. This time her fears turned out to be pointless since the glider and its occupant took a hard landing. She watched as Joe pulled the occupant from the glider. She jumped down and began to stomp down the fire that was threatening to spread. Suddenly she was joined by the four ranch hand trainees who pulled the grey glider chute over the fire and smothered it.

Joe arrived just as the glider more or less crashed directly into the ground. He watched as the gas from the engine immediately caught fire. He focused on pulling the unconscious occupant from the glider and getting his helmet off. The surprise was that it was a woman. He had no idea who she was. He checked to see in what condition she was in and realized that she had a broken arm, a broken leg and most likely might have internal injuries.

Lydia located the scoped rifle and took it over to the crashed para glider. She waved up to Less and Jack who wagged their gliders and headed back toward the ranch house.

Joe knew that the rest of the day was going to be spent on finding out who the woman in the glider was and who she might be working with. He also knew that once again he had people that he did not know wanting him dead.

15 At Least Seven

16

Retribution for Success

Events around the Admiral never seem to be dull and I, Laki always look forward to his next adventure. I found it interesting that when the Admiral was asked by Uncle Ted how many more journeys the Admiral planned to lead the reply was, "at least seven."

It is also on record that on his return to Madorite he was attacked not because of political reasons but because of the success he was having. In my investigations I discovered that his successes had upset the financial markets on Earth to the extent that several large companies failed due to their refusal to take into account the impact of trade that would be feasible from Earth to worlds across the galaxies. I learned that this was not trade in physical goods but trade in knowledge, computer programing, internet, network, and power systems design. The ability to leverage the technical capabilities was not properly assessed. My additional learning was that the final straw was when AI came on the scene and altered all the previous technical interrelationships.

16 Retribution for Success

Records show that the Admiral was clueless about the matters that had caused several very wealthy and powerful individuals who had concluded that by killing him the disruption would at least for a time settle down and allow them to continue to increase their personal wealth. The records suggest that those individuals never admitted their complicity in the attempted assassination of the Admiral but commented that the rate of change he had caused had exceeded what the business markets could handle, and something had to be done to slow things down.

The Admiral had a small but very loyal set of supportive followers that remained on Earth who informed him of what the situation was. I learned that this information did not reach him directly but came through Captain Samantha Westerfield, who got the information from her parents. It came through Darian's parents. And very close to home it came from Lydia's parents and from her brother Jarad who arrived a few days after the attack on Madorite. He had accepted the position of Ranch Operations Manager for Rear Admirals Jorge Martines and Gerald Delaney. His role was to oversees all aspects of a ranch's daily operations, ensuring efficient and effective management of livestock, land, and resources, while also managing the ranch hands. His personal diary clearly states that it was a dream come true for him. It stated that it was a dream that came to life back on the ranch on Earth during his high school senior year.

The Gentle Eye

It is recorded that upon learning of the source of the attacks the Admiral took a quick trip back to Earth and engaged his old friend the Cosmos base security officer, Doug Hasterly, and asked him to investigate the people that had instigated the assassination attempt. If there was solid incriminating evidence he authorized Doug to instigated economic sanctions against those individuals. The record shows that indeed that is what happened. I learned that what was often overlooked was that the Admiral had a bottomless supply of gold that was being mined on his Madorite ranch which made him as rich as all the combined billionaires on Earth. This was a surprise for me as the reality of how principally disciplined the Admiral was hit me. He was not vengeful, but he was also not going to allow unprincipled billionaires to escape a punishment of their own doing. He was going to make sure they got a taste of their own medicine. But it was medicine that would apply pain and was not a punishment of death.

But let me refocus on the dynamic atmosphere that was so uplifting on the four ranches on Madorite. I personally was rooting for all four ranches. The subsequent records indicate that many other ranches were established but the first four were the largest and most successful. The Three Green Caps Ranch was about twice the size of each of the other three but all of them were larger than subsequent ranches.

The Tabletop Ranch was the one that had the most unique feature and was the ranch that had its two partners living above the clouds. The two buddies had the unique distinction of having the most small lakes on the property. The two buddies stocked each lake with a specific type of fish and produced roughly sixty percent of all the fish sold on Madorite.

And the Hilo One Ranch had the unique distinction of having the a plateau that made up eighty percent of the ranch. Where the Tabletop Ranch went high into the sky the Hilo One Ranch had the distinction of being a plateau that was a low tabletop that covered roughly one hundred square miles.

Let me conclude this reporting with letting you know that the Admiral was heavily committed to the success of all the ranches. He made sure that Uncle Ted and his father had all the resources they needed to make the four ranches successful.

I have come to the conclusion that having the Admiral as a neighbor was to truly have the best neighbor possible.

****

Joe looked up and watched as Less and Jack made a circle. He swirled his finger like a hilo copter blade hoping they would get the idea that he wanted the hilo flown out. He watched as Jack swirled his finger and pointed back toward the ranch house and turned on his motor and headed that way. Less swayed his glider and followed Jack.

Joe focused back on the badly injured woman and pulled her broken leg straight and then used a piece of the glider as a splint. He then placed her broken arm across her chest. He used his knife to cut a strip off the grey chute to make a sling to hold her arm. He took another strip and wrapped her legs together so that the good leg provided support.

Lydia watched Joe doing a great job in getting the wounded woman ready for transport. She hoped that Less and Jack had understood what Joe had signaled to them. She was just getting ready to tell the four hands to return to the ranch when she heard the hilo. She was pleased at how fast the turnaround had been. She shielded her eyes with her hand and was able to make out the hilo coming fast and flying close to the ground.

Jack had led the way back to the ranch house and was glad that the hilo was still on the ground. He landed his glider, ran to the house, and found that Lily and Lev were still in the kitchen chatting with Uncle Ted. When they heard what had happened the two of them jumped up and followed him to the hilo. Before taking off he watched as they folded up most of the seating and took out a first aid kit from the luggage compartment. He then jumped in and was followed by Less.

Uncle Ted and Trey understood that the two had downed a person flying in a hang glider who needed to be transported to the hospital. Ted asked if anyone else had been hurt. He was relieved that Less and Jack thought that no one else was hurt.

Lily was flying first seat and Lev had taken the copilot position so he could get out immediately upon landing. He asked Jack for the direction they should fly.

Jack pointed his arm and said to go toward the highest of the three peaks.

Lily flew fast and low across the plain towards the peak. She spotted the grey-yellow collapsed chute in the center of a black burnt area and landed near it.

Lev jumped out and took the folding body board, head protector and the first aid kit and went over to where Joe was kneeling next to a body.

Lydia watched the hilo land and Lev jump out and bring the rescue gear to where Joe was kneeling next to the female attacker. She wondered who she might be and who she was working for. She asked one of the new hands to go back to the house and bring back the wagon so the glider could be removed from the field.

Lev opened the body board and locked it before getting the woman strapped to it. His quick assessment of her condition impressed him by what Joe had done with nothing but the chute material and a metal rod that was part of the glider. He gave the woman a shot to keep her slightly out so that she would not be in pain.

He then rolled her onto the board and strapped her down and put a head protector on her. He called over two of the ranch hands that were standing and watching and had them help him pick up the board and carry it to the hilo.

By the time the woman was in the hilo, Lydia could see the wagon coming across the plain. She had the parachute disconnected from the crumpled frame of the motor and propeller of the glider. She let Joe know that she would supervise the removal of the glider. She handed him the empty rifle that the woman had used and a small bag that had the bullets in it.

Less took the rifle from Joe and put it in the baggage compartment. He said that he and Jack would fly in with the hilo and get their security team to check out who the woman was. He said that he had seen her around and recognized her because she had a lightening tattoo on her neck that he had spotted before.

Jack said that she had to work somewhere on the base, and it probably would not take them long to find out who she was. He added that he doubted that she had acted on her own.

Joe nodded, agreed, and said that he was going to come along in case she regained consciousness. He wanted to see if they could get the name of who had hired her. He had little interest in prosecuting her except for the fact that she had been willing to kill him. He was very interested why she would have been willing to do so since even if she had been successful she would most likely have been caught.

On the flight to the hospital the woman woke up and asked what had happened. Joe said that her glider had crashed, and she had a broken leg and arm. He asked for her name and learned that she was Rasvan Cazacu.

He then asked who had hired her. She said that it was a man who promised that she would get a million dollars, and her parents would get a lifetime residency at a very good retirement community in Florida. She had agreed to the assassination once her parents were in the retirement home. She had asked why someone would want to assassinate someone who was traveling the universe discovering other worlds with people on them and had learned that the person putting up the money was taking a hit on the wealth he had amassed because of the change in the world's economy.

Joe thanked her for the information and asked if she had any idea who the wealthy man might be. He watched as she tried to shake her head and said that the only thing she had learned was that he was the world's largest dealer in gold mining.

Joe smiled and thought about Doug and his IT team back on the Cosmos Earth Base at Lakland. He figured he had enough information that Doug would be able to identify who that gold dealer was.

Once they got to the hospital Jess said that he and Jack would get in touch with their old boss and find out who had put up the money for the assassination. He then asked what Joe planned to do once he had a name.

Joe smiled and said that he was going to financially kick that person in the teeth. Jess should let Doug know that he had as much money as he needed to take any action that would in essence financially assassinate that person.

He added that once they had a name he would personally meet with Doug and anyone else who he had selected to design a takedown strategy. He wanted the person who he was going to kick to know who was doing the kicking.

Jack said that might take millions of dollars.

Joe nodded and smiled as he thought about the almost solid gold vein that he and Lydia mined every time they vacationed on the ranch. It was a gold streak that was solid gold that was at least a foot thick and was in a long crevasse along the side of one of the hills that surrounded the valley with his and Lydia's skinny dipping lake. They had so far mined almost a billion dollars that they had Uncle Ted and his father investing in the stock market on Earth and buying property on Madorite and Nivian. They owned the ranch outright; they owned the helicopter that Lily and Lev flew. Their ranch was not only the place they came to relax, but it was also the place they came to play gold miners and investment tycoons.

Lydia was back on the ranch discussing how the establishment of the ranch was coming. She was interested in the livestock, and all the gardens that she had so far seen only from the air.

Uncle Ted shared that he and Trey had taken a slightly different tack from what they had done on Earth where they were still focused almost entirely on raising cattle. They were taking a broader approach on the Three Green Caps Ranch.

16 Retribution for Success

Raising Cattle was still number one, but they were also raising and harvesting fish and clams, they were establishing green houses, and raising a mix of vegetables, they had planted several large grape vineyards. They had apple, tangerine, pear, and cherry tree orchards located around the ranch. The ranch would eventually have about fifty workers tending to all of the new plantings and efforts.

Lydia let out a low whistle and said that she was impressed with what they were doing and wondered when the first fruit would be ready to enjoy. She knew that Jorge and Jerry were resourcing the fruits and vegetables available on the Cosmos ships mostly from the Earth. They were looking at the other planets for similar produce but that would take a few years to get into place since each fruit or vegetable had to be tested out to ensure that they were compatible to the Cosmos personnel. She would love to have access to as much as the ranch could raise.

Uncle Ted chuckled and said that he already had a contract with Jorge who had expressed his desire to get as much of everything as possible. Their was a demand that currently exceeded supply. It made it easy to consider expanding all the gardens and orchards.

Joe was pleased with the speed that Doug responded to his request to identify the person who had hired the would be assassin. He scheduled a day to meet with him and suggested they meet at the ranch on Earth. This would let him mix in a little fishing and let him see how the ranch he had grown up on was doing.

The Gentle Eye

Doug arrived for the meeting with three other people. He introduced one of them as a leading market investment guru. The second person was a social media influencer that dealt with gossip about various famous personalities. The third person was an investigator specializing in personal surveillance. He then shared that the team had laid out a three prong plan. First, they would set up investment scenarios that would publicly set sell short targets on the companies owned by the person they were targeting, and they would simultaneously get the social media hype to be about the poor condition of the companies owned and operated by the individual that would drive down the value of that stock. The two would work the system to see if they could have the negative effect they were seeking. The investigator would be gathering information about what went on in the person's private life. If there was any damaging behavior it would be fed into the social media narrative.

Joe smiled, nodded, and said that he wanted all of their action to be kept on the legal side. He asked how long it would be before they had an idea if the actions were taking effect. He was surprised to learn that it could be in as little as a few weeks, or it might drag out to a year.

He thanked Doug and the team that he had set up and asked them if they cared to end the day by doing some fishing at his favorite fishing hole. He also invited them all out to his ranch on Madorite once they had successfully implemented their plan.

17

Success Celebration

As always, I, Laki am pleased with the approach that the Admiral chose to recognize all the people in the Cosmos Space Force. He demonstrated his detailed knowledge of every position on the Cosmos spaceships and made a point of recognizing their contributions.

When I say recognize, I am speaking of giving social recognition, giving work recognition through promotions, and giving significant financial bonuses. It also reminded me that he operated the Cosmos organization on a flat pay scale. So, when he announced a ten percent pay raise it meant everyone was rewarded.

It was also impressive that the Admiral recalled the bravery, the dedication to the excellence that he worked so hard for the entire organization to have down to details like the person who had found a missile in storage that had a loose strap. He recognized that person and awarded her a cash prize with the hope that she would use it on her next vacation that he was also granting her. The list of such minor details is too long to go through but almost every individual was recognized in some fashion.

The only other reward that is worth mentioning because it received a rousing, Voya, Voya, Voya shout out from all the Cosmos crew members was the ones given to the Chef's for the great meals that they consistently served all of the crews.

It is also interesting how he handled the selection of where the Cosmos ships would go next. I leave this for you to find out.

****

Joe return from the ranch on Earth to his Three Green Caps ranch on Madorite determined to continue the vacation he had planned. On his return, Uncle Ted offered to tour him on all the new features that the ranch was branching into. Joe said that he was eager to see what Uncle Ted and his father were up to.

Lydia nodded and added that she was also eager and ask what the best way to see it all.

Lily and Lev were standing by the hilo when the four walked out of the house. They said that they were as eager to see the different gardens, greenhouses, orchards, and grape vineyards. They just needed the coordinates of each location, and they would get them all there in a timely manner.

Uncle Ted suggested that they travel to the apple orchard that was the farthest away and work their way back toward the house.

Trey smiled and said that the way back was going to be more like a honeybee traveling from flower to flower in an apparent random manner because each orchard was in a separate valley or canyon, and they were more or less randomly scattered across the ranch.

The Gentle Eye

Lydia asked if there was a topographical map of the ranch and learned that there was not. She said that she was going to ask one of the Cosmos ships that were in orbit to take some pictures of the ranch so that in the future they could mark where each orchards were located.

Uncle Ted said that the selection of apples would be limited to Honeycrisp, Gala, Fuji, Red Delicious and Golden Delicious. All the trees were doing well and the biggest challenge they had was that there were no bees to help in doing the pollinating. He had worked with a couple of engineers in the Cosmos labs to develop a battery powered fan that was used to blow from one tree to another to pollinate the flowers.

Trey commented that they would have plenty of apples but that unlike bee pollinated trees, feeding the riders and horses required to pollinate the six large orchards it made each apple ten time as expensive as the ones grown on Earth. He added it was no different with the other fruit trees and grape orchards.

Joe asked what other fruits were being grown.

His father answered that they had a couple of pear orchards and one apricot orchard.

The hilo flights to each of the groves went smoothly and by lunchtime Lydia had accumulated a bowl full of slightly green apples and one bunch of ripe white grapes that she had found. She commented that she was looking forward to getting the first ripened fruit sent to the Terra so she could feed her dreams of returning to the ranch.

The surprise came when they flew into the canyon where the Apricot orchard was located. Many of the apricot fruits were ripe.

Joe asked if there were any plans for getting cherry trees, peach, or plum trees.

Trey replied that those were all currently growing in one of the greenhouses in what he and Ted called the Greenhouse valley.

By the time the sun was setting in the East, they were all ready for a relaxing evening meal on the front deck.

The next day, their last day on the ranch, Joe, and Lydia rode to their swimming lake where after a leisurely swim, they each mined a bag full of gold and then enjoyed a picnic lunch.

They returned to the house where they sat in the family room relaxing until it was time for dinner.

Uncle Ted shared that the highlight of the dinner was going to be the desert. He had prepared a truly great apple pie by par-cooking the apples using a combination of the tart and sweet apple varieties. He added that the flour made from some of the wheat they had grown, and the flour made with the seeds of the locally abundant grasses created one of the best flaky and tasty crusts.

He then added that the apricots had been used to create a Mascarpone and caramelized apricot layered sponge cake. The Mascarpone had been made using the cream from the small herd of milk cows that he kept in the field outside of the barn.

He had caramelized the apricots by letting them cook slowly until most of the moisture had boiled off so that the cake would not get soggy. He pointed out that usually he used an array of fruit but this time he was keeping to what he had on hand.

Uncle Ted made a point of preparing the main plates for each person. He kept the portions small so that everyone would have plenty of space for desert. He had spent most of his time getting that prepared to what he hoped was perfection. The surprise that he had not mentioned was that he had also made ice cream in vanilla, apple, and apricot flavors to accompany the desert. The effort took the help of all the ranch hands since he had made sure that enough was being prepared for everyone.

Desert indeed was the highlight. Lydia found it hard to keep from stuffing herself. The ice cream made each bite a special sensation as its sweetness merged with the rest of the mouthwatering flavor of either the pie or the cake. She decided that the apricot ice cream definitely was the favorite though the tart apple ice cream was a close second.

The next day, as they got ready to fly to the Cosmos base to return to the Terra both she and Joe had another serving of dessert for breakfast. She walked to the hilo with a bowl of apricot ice cream to eat on the way.

21 Completion and Next Steps

Joe had two coolers with the deserts and ice cream that were for Jorge and Jerry. He wished he could take some out to the Terra. He decided that one of the challenges he was going to present to Gentle Eye was how to modify the Door transport system to also transport non biological elements.

Both Jorge and Jerry accepted their cooler and said that they would be looking forward to enjoying it after dinner that evening.

Once on the Terra, Joe called for an all hands meeting for the next day.

Joe knew that his call for an all hands meeting made everyone wonder what was happening. He wanted to seize the moment and remind everyone of all the great work they had been a part of, and he wanted everyone to immediately get into the mood. He began by asking if anyone recalled what panspermia meant. There was a moment of silence so he proceeded to remind everyone that it was the theory that life may have originated elsewhere in the universe and reached Earth by space travel. That had been the theory they had all set out together to prove or disprove. He chuckled and added that even his Captains had doubted that theory but they all knew now that the theory had been true.

He then announced that everyone would receive a bonus of one thousand dollars for having hung in there and been part of proving it true.

He heard the now famous, "Voya, Voya, Voya," refrain throughout all ships.

Joe then reminded everyone about their less than friendly greeting by the humans on the fifth planet where they had learned the secret of creating the gravity that they were now enjoying on every Cosmos ship and where they had picked up the design of their current very powerful rocket engines. He thanked all the engineers and other people that had rapidly built and installed that technology on their only missile shaped ship, the ISF Cosmos Javelin that ultimately became the home for the United Intergalactic Worlds Organization. He thanked everyone for their brave actions and the swift incorporation of that new technical capability. He announced that everyone was getting a battle ribbon with the number five on it. That ribbon would always be good for one free drink at any Cosmos bar.

Once again Joe heard, "Voya, Voya, Voya."

He then announced two special awards to the two current fighter pilots that had saved his and Captain Tabata's lives and who recently had located their new Cosmos member Gentle Eye and that he was giving them the award of having Apple, Pear and Peach orchards planted on their ranch on Madorite.

Joe heard the cheers came from the fighter pilot group, but it was broadcast through all the ships.

He then asked everyone to put on their neural head gear because he was going to recognize the person who had found the plans for it and who had become the best hacker in the fleet and had saved their bacon multiple times.

He asked Elisha to stand to a be recognized and then he said that he wanted to thank his Neural Ranch neighbor for having become the most talented hacker in the Universe. He continued that was not all. She was also the person that saved their bacon when they faced the Kelapan warship by disabling its computer control system. She also lifted the plans for the neural mind link that was now in common use across the Cosmos fleet. He then added a piece of information that he had not even shared with Lydia. He said that Elisha was a participant in the flight of the Kodho as it tried to escape the heat wave of the dying red sun. She had used her hacking skills to reach in and boost the output of the Kodho's light speed engines that gave it that crucial boost as the heat wave burned its tail. He then announced that not only was she now the proud owner of a ranch next to his, but she had earned a second star on her uniform.

This time he could hear the, "Voya, Voya, Voya," through his neural link. He also watched as Lydia shook her head, pointed at him, and walked over to Elisha and embraced her.

Elisha pointed at him just as Lydia had and she too shook her head. Until that moment she had thought that her actions had gone unnoticed.

It was clear to Joe that both of them had tears in their eyes and he was sure they were both living those crucial moments when it seemed that the Kodho was not going to make it.

He had long ago accepted the fact that the successful outcome of that Kodho run was his reward for life.

He then announced that the Kodho would be honored with two stars as well to commemorate its successful run ahead of the dying sun.

He could hear Captain Yang lead the, "Voya, Voya, Voya," cry for his ship.

He then reminded everyone of the sad situation they found the condition on the planet Mirabiro and the effort that the entire Cosmos fleet was still carrying out to help get that planet reestablished. He said that he was having a statue that displayed all the names of all Cosmos personnel built and delivered as a gift to Mirabiro.

Once again he received a "Voya, Voya, Voya," from the Cosmos members.

He then asked if everyone more recently recalled their search for the answer to his demand for the answer to WHY. Why would a sentient civilization try to destroy the star of another sentient civilization.

He remined everyone of what that answer was and the fact that they had found a sentient civilization that was entirely computer based. They had found the answer to WHY and they had successfully defeated those computers in a hard-fought battle, and they had discovered one computer that had done the honorable thing and turned itself off to prevent it from being used to discover more biological sentient civilizations that the supercomputers would destroy.

They had discovered Gentle Eye. In turn he pointed out that Gently Eye had saved all of them by shutting down a weapon meant to destroy planets. He had saved their bacon. He then announced that he was promoting Gently Eye to the position of Rear Admiral.

There was a "Voya, Voya, Voya," heard throughout the ships. But Joe knew that the message he received from Gentle Eye was only for him.

Gentle Eye let him know that he could not experience tears, he could only imagine love, but he knew that his devotion would always be to him.

Joe said that he had arranged what would be a special lunch that featured steak from his ranch or fish and fresh fruit that had been sent up by Uncle Ted and his father.

That got a, "Voya, Voya, Voya," and afterwards he closed the meeting.

After the meeting he gathered the Captains, Tom, H[3], Linda and Gentle Eye and asked where they were going next.

The End

About the Author

Ronald E. Mueller
remwriter95@gmail.com

Ron grew up in what is now Flint River State Park in Southeast Iowa. The 170-year-old house Ron lived in is built into a hillside. It faces a 125-foot-high cliff towering over the little Flint River. The house and the land talked to him about; the passing of time, the struggle to conquer the land, the struggles people faced and the wonder of nature.

He climbed the cliffs, crawled into the caves, dove from the swimming rock, collected clams from the bottom of the pond, gigged and skinned frogs for their legs. He trapped muskrats for fur, hunted raccoon in the dead of night, and with only a stick hunted rabbits in the dead of winter.

His young life was outdoors, and nature tested him.

He walked to a one room stone schoolhouse uphill both ways. A stern but warm-hearted teacher, Mrs. Henry was instrumental in shaping his character as she shepherded him from the fourth to the eighth grade. A Montessori before its time. It was a wonderful way to grow up.

His experiences inter-twined with snippets of fantasy lend themselves to the adventures he leads the reader through.

Characters in the Stories

Jorge	Martinez	Rear Admiral Leading the effort Lakland Airforce base
Jimena	Martinez	Jorge's wife
Lydia	Jade Tabata	Main characters. Joe's companion
Joe	Pender Elsinger	main character Five Star Admiral
Uncle Ted	Stratford	Like a second father to Joe
Trey	Elsinger	Joe's father
Jarad	Tabata	Lydia's younger brother
Tui	White Koi	Name of Lydia's horse
La	black Koi	Name of Joe's horse
Three Green Caps Ranch		Joe and Lydia Emelio foreman
The Tabletop Ranch		Less and Jake Balem Menchu foreman
Two Buddies Ranch		Jorge and Jerry Jarad Tabata foreman
Hilo One Ranch		Tyler and Veetry
Balam	Menchú	youngest ranch hand - foreman on the Table Top
Harold	Hatfield Hastly	H³ key character mate to Yara
Yara	Zepfly	Captain H³ mate
Lacey	McAdam	US President then Captain
Craig	Lebak	President
General Jerald	Delaney	USMC-> Rear Admiral
Doug	Hasterly	Security officer
Linda	Hall	Genius Scientist
Tom	Hall	Genius Scientist
Darian		Second person sent through the door
Samantha	Westerfield	Darians mate
Liên	Ngoc Westerfield	Mother
Aiden	Westerfield	Father
Jacqueline		Jackie psychologist
Bilian	Phene	DNA analyst
Cosmos Odyssey	Cpt Yara	Destroyed, replaced with Odyssey II
Cosmos Voyager	Cpt Lydia	Joe's name for the second Doorship to be converted
Cosmos Endeavor	Cpt Samantha	Named after HMS Endeavor Explorer
Cosmos Enabler	Cpt Julius Wilsmith	Door deployer for Planet resettlement
Cosmos Empowerer	Cpt Jeffery Yang	Equipment Deployer for building planet infrastructure
Cosmos Optimizer	Cpt Ned Saters	Door deployer for Planet resettlement
Cosmos Ambassador	Cpt Lacey McAdam	7th ship but fourth ship in the rotation of the Cosmos Triad.
Cosmos Quartet	four cosmos ships hooked together as one.	
Cosmos Javelin		New rocket shaped ship with gravity generators, extensive weaponry
ISF Cosmos Sphere One	becomes the Terra	
VOYA	Hurrah	Space Force equivalent of Marine Orah
Sparrow system		small spear like missiles
Fabio	Maria-Gonzalez	cow hand-Chef on the USS Cosmos Endeavor
Emiliano	Ayala.	ranch supervisor Chef on the USS Cosmos Empower
Alvaro	Becerra	cow hand-Chef on the USS Cosmos Optimizer
Claude	Laurent	French Chef in the White House-on the USS Cosmos Odessey
Anika	Van Dijk	Dutch Chef on the USS Cosmos Voyager
Ned	Saters	US Navy captain recruited into the force.
Julious	Wilsmith	Airforce Major recommended by Jorge
Elisha	Sands	Top hacker on the Voyager
Kaden-Amile	Kashanti	New linguist on board the Voyager
Tyler	Randle	Older Hilo Pilot
Veetry	Rao	Younger Hilo Pilot
Lily		partner pilots
Lev		partner pilots
Less		Biker looking member of security team

Characters in the Story

Jack		Biker looking member of security team
Rasvan	Cazacu	Romanian descent who tried to kill Joe
Sir Fergus	Angus Barcley	Scottish Linguist joins the team
Morag	Barcley	wife to Sir Barcley
Lanial	Datus	New Hilo pilot
Maylee	Tran	New female Hilo pilot
Nojus	Vilkas	organizer of the attack on Joe
Draco (Wŭ)		fifth planet populated by Dinosaurs
Scorp		Fifth planet leader
Joba		Mate of fifth planet leader
Juss		Linguist on Wu
Anura		Seventh Planet - frog like people
Aeolia		the eighth planet in the system
Hurlians		The hateful ones
Hurlian		Name of the planet
Naxtly		sixth planet
Naxlians		What the beings called themselves.
Sinkat	Planet	Ray of light
Kahel	Star	Orange
Zielony		fifth planet in the Kahel system
First Planet		
Niam		Earth like Planet Found by Joe and team
Izuba		Name of the red sun
Niamians		what the beings called themselves
Region of Space	**Qualite** (X)	the new galaxy
Star	**Izulite** (X)	the new star
Planet	1. Tazurite	the new planets
	2. Rarimar	
	3. Dazuli	
	4. Nivian	
	5. Madorite	Planet base for Intergalactic force
	6. Leridia	
Rilagan		Planet in the Salidan system
Datax	Usadan	Rilagan Commander of the vessel
		Ship's name of an almost invincible
Invictus		sentinel spaceship
grenden units		powered the ships
Castor		contact on Rilagan
Sikatians		the beings on the planet Sinkat
Kahel		Star
Sinkat		Planet number four
Freya		tenth Rilagan Avenger
Król Wysoki		High Lord ruler of Sinkat
Zielony		Planet number five
Męski		
Morsă	Cading	Commander of Alien vessels
	Panglima	
	peluru berpandu	Missiles
	yoke	juk
Vyfde	fifth plane	
Agtste	eight planet	
Second planet		
Bintang		Outie Star
Gaja	Outie planet	Outie Planet with Earth like beings.
Zacker		Being on Gaja
Mensia		Human
Melidia	Mecally	Leader of leadership council
Third Planet		
Endilo		In command of the three ship

Aggla		sixth planet
Edalia		fourth planets name
Iliady		star's name
Fourth Planet		
Rately		In command of the spaceship
Sinket		Name of the Star
Witneia		Name fifth planet
Fifth Planet		
Kelima		fifth planet
Bintang		Star of system
Riccart		Commander of triad leadership
Tirayidi		Leaders of the ship
Dili		Ships Name
Yu'ēsi'ēsi Dili		Ships designation
pilaniki		unit of time = a second
Leland		loyal ship mate
Delan		loyal ship mate
Redan		female worker
Sixth planet		
Mangkas	Kesengguan	Commander of Sixth colony space ship
Nambelas		son
Bini		wife
Bola Satu		ship Sphere number one
Keterubah		Planet of humans in the sixth planet
Mata Panas		Sun of the sixth colony
Seventh Planet		
Mirabiro		Seventh Planet
Ceng		Star
Ngati		Person on planet that was a local leader
Dhako		Mate to that person
Nyathin		Child of the two
Harikiamat		Doomsday vault
Eighth Planet		
Kelapan		Eighth planet
Sulwe		Star
Keadilan		Commander or spherical battleship
Bola		Name of the Eighth planet sphere
Planet that attacked the Eighth		
Jomaoko		Planet
Chieng'		Star
Dainoso		Leader of the Jamaokons
Ochiagha		Commander of the Jamaokon fleet
Janekmar		Planet killer weapon
Ninth Planet		
Maraburo		Nineth planet
Kpakpan		Star
Laki	Anak	The narrator lead in for each chapter
Kodho		Name of seeding starship.
Jaktus	Producy	Leadership Council Leader
Azwanú		Clever one Equivalent of Engineer
Diḑeḑiḑe.		Map Maker Equivalent of Geography
Ayikungban		Ground Tracker Equivalent to Geologist
Ziquratum		High builder Equivalent to Architect
Ragegita		Finder of the old way Equiv to Historian
Bekee		The Maraburan equivalent to English
Ecals		Star
Ader		Planet
Aderals		People of the attacking planet
Ucigaş		Sheep behemoth Spaceship.

Characters in the Story

Slaadair	commander on the behemoth
Leus	Fourth planet Sheep
Trepus	Fifth planet Wolves
Madadh	Wolf leader
Intergalactic Space Force	
United Intergalactic Worlds Organization	

Published by: Around the World Publishing LLC.

QR Links to
ATWP.US web site

www.ingramcontent.com/pod-product-compliance
Lightning Source LLC
Chambersburg PA
CBHW070535100726
47907CB00004B/1127